D1398606

In *Popsicle Fish*, *Murphy reflects on lessons from his everyday experience with his young sons. There's a lot for fathers to take away from his essays. Several gave me goosebumps. All made me feel more human. The book reminded me that children are great teachers—they can help us know ourselves—and the most simple interactions with them can be profound. I remembered times of connection with my own children, and vowed to find ways to stay connected. For that, I thank Michael Murphy and his sons.*

Fred P. Piercy, Ph.D.
Program Director at Purdue University
Department of Child Development and Family Studies

Popsicle Fish reaches deep down into the pockets of every parent's laughs and wishes, heartaches and hopes, and pulls out fistfuls of wisdom and love. Reading Popsicle Fish is like browsing through your family album, declaring, "Yes, I remember that!" and discovering that the father he discusses is you, the children in the stories are yours, and the message is for everybody. Like all family albums, you will hold onto this one forever.

Dr. Paul Coleman, Psy.D., Clinical Psychologist
Author of *The 30 Secrets of Happily Married Couples*

Popsicle Fish

Tales of Fathering

By Michael J. Murphy, Ed.D.

Illustrations by Susanna Hepburn Kravitz

Foreword by Jack Canfield
Co-Author of *Chicken Soup for the Soul*

HEALTH PRESS
Santa Fe, New Mexico

Photo by Robert R. Tucker

Copyright 1996 by Michael J. Murphy, Ed.D.

Published by Health Press
P.O. Drawer 1388
Santa Fe, NM 87504

10 9 8 7 6 5 4 3 2

Library of Congress Cataloging in Publication Data

ISBN 0-929173-23-6

Illustrations by Susanna Hepburn Kravitz

They do not understand how that which separates
unites with itself. It is a harmony of oppositions, as in
the case of the bow and of the lyre.

Heracletus of Ephesus
Circa 500 B.C.

TABLE OF CONTENTS

ACKNOWLEDGMENTS

For a book such as this the list of those to whom to express gratitude must begin small and expand to include the whole universe, for the material that comprises it—my perplexing, laughable and heartrending experiences as a father—was itself first and foremost a grand gift from the gods to me.

The beautiful places we have lived deserve first mention, for they provided the context for it all: the wooded hills of Vermont and western Massachusetts, whose cold refreshing rivers and sharp winter winds kept my mind alert; the wide-rolling Texas plains, whose open skies bring into sharp relief even the most mundane events, will always seem like home to me; and the wind-blown shore of Cape Cod, with its strangely slanted orange afternoon light, strikes me silent so that at other moments I might have recourse to words.

The people I have met in these places—clients encountered in the profoundest sincerity late at night in a hospital emergency room; colleagues who during moments of pure idealism have shared a common struggle to lend some note of peace or light to a community, and the many momentary mentors from Commerce, Texas, to North Adams, Massachusetts, who have done me the honor of sharing themselves with me—have my deepest appreciation. You probably don't know who you are, but nonetheless I must let you know that you are remembered.

I owe to my mother and father the most powerful lessons in clear-eyed willingness to persevere; to my sisters and brothers the deep sense that balancing conflict is a unity that can be relied upon to appear at the most unexpected—and important—moments. You allowed me to be a little strange and to thrive nonetheless, and that tilting gave my vision whatever new slant it might possess today.

I want to express my deep appreciation to my oldest son Benjamin for patiently providing me with the opportunity to learn what it means to be a father. His shining spirit is testament to his capacity to persevre, despite my bumbling efforts.

I want to thank Jack Canfield, whose sincerity and openness to my work played a large part in setting this whole process in motion, in ways that I will someday explain over the long-discussed cup of coffee.

The members of the Family Consultation Team, both past and present, have shared the magical chemistry that happens when caring is made real. Lois Callahan and Jo D. Pockette-Fralich have shared lessons of the heart and mind. And Garry McKeon—er, MacKoul—in addition to being one of the last pure appreciators is a most treasured friend.

Many thanks to Susanna Hepburn Kravitz, who as illustrator took the risk of leaping upon an already fast-moving train. Your openness is exceeded only by your talent, which I am pleased to play some small part in bringing to the world.

My deep appreciation as well goes out to Kathleen Schwartz of Health Press, whose care and sensitivity to my work has at times exceeded my own. Your competence and disciplined passion for service, as well as your willingness to take a flier on an unknown writer, should be a model for all in the publishing world.

My gratitude to my children will hopefully be amply communicated by this book itself. They have challenged me to experience them. This book is my reply.

Finally, my wife Miriam, through her great honesty and courage, has allowed me to see that the adventure of the family need not be limited by my paltry Irish imagination. There were moments when we only knew how good it was going to be by how bad it was. You made it all possible, and, to my great benefit, you didn't make it too easy.

FOREWORD

As Mark Victor Hansen and I were compiling the stories for our book *Chicken Soup for the Soul*, we were delighted to discover and include a wonderful piece by Michael Murphy. I had never met Michael Murphy—except through his writings in the *Family Therapy Networker* magazine—but over the years of reading his articles I had fallen in love with him. Not romantically, of course, but as a fellow sensitive and loving father who thinks deeply and reflectively about himself and his role as a father. He is, as I told my wife, "a good man!"

He is a man with a big dream, a big heart, and a desire to truly make a difference. His rich background as a marriage and family therapist, forensic psychologist, lecturer, men's group facilitator, author, and father has enabled him to intimately see and share in the challenges facing all families today. He has seen the ravages of child abuse and other violence, and he sees a country that is in dire need of fathering.

I always feel moved, warm, more full, and more at peace with myself and my humanity whenever I finish one of Michael's stories. Playing a part in bringing Michael's writings to an audience of more than four million people has brought me great joy. Many, many people have commented to me about how much they were touched by Michael's story. Now I am excited to have the honor of introducing Michael's first book, *Popsicle Fish: Tales of Fathering*.

Popsicle Fish makes a radical contribution in acknowledging the differences between fathering and mothering. Michael's long overdue message is that it's okay for fathers to parent differently than mothers. What fathers and mothers bring to parenting are essential to a child's development, and this book can serve as a wonderful bridge between the sexes and the generations. It provides a window through which both women and men can explore and develop a deep respect for the masculine art of fathering.

Through *Popsicle Fish* Michael redefines fatherhood, not in terms of money, political power, or social dominance but rather in terms of our humanity. Insofar as fathering is a vital aspect of one's manhood, this book is an essential step in the process of redefining the term "male power."

Working with men incarcerated for crimes of violence, Michael has seen an army of unfathered and undeveloped young men. Because of this experience he offers *Popsicle Fish* as a loving yet powerful message that fathering is a unique and essential masculine task. Unique—as every father's relationship with his child is unique; and essential—because it brings out in each child what no other relationship can.

The intensity and depth of Michael's professional and personal experience have made these pages a delightful reading treasure. You are bound to find yourself experiencing the full spectrum of your emotions, from laughter to tears. Michael's prose is gracefully guided by his sensitivity to language, rhythm, and humanity. His ability to disclose his own vulnerabilities and allow difficult and profound questions to remain illuminated but unanswered will no doubt touch your heart as it has touched mine many times.

As you prepare to read this magical journey into fatherhood, let me offer you this last piece of advice: One must digest *Popsicle Fish* even more slowly than one digests *Chicken Soup*. After all, chicken soup is a well-known soother for an upset system, but Popsicle Fish, well. . . . As I urge my readers, don't hurry through this book. Take the time to savor each story and reflect deeply upon the meaning it has for you as a parent. Take the time to engage each and every story with your whole being. Remember to listen to the words with your heart as well as your mind. You are in for a wonderful treat. Enjoy it.

Jack Canfield
Co-Author, *Chicken Soup for the Soul*

INTRODUCTION

Just the other day four-year-old Aaron was talking about some topic of great meaning to him—the names of the cartoon heroes of the moment or their complex powers—when I was suddenly moved to squeeze him in my arms and tell him how much I love him. As I released him, he turned his small face up toward mine and spoke with great seriousness.

"Dad," he said. "You love me even when you get mad at me and yell at me, don't you?"

Discerning the correct answer to this question was not a difficult task, though it was hard to withstand the way my heart reached out to this little person who had given me a great gift—the gift of sharing with perfect honesty how much it meant to him to mean something to me.

It wasn't always this way. As a guy who grew up as guys do in our culture I learned to act as if I didn't have an emotional life. Men, I thought, were meant to do things, and emotions interfere with accomplishment. As a being who was young, inadequate, and male, I yearned to be free of feelings. Feelings were for women, and that was the reason why for the longest time I could only feel complete when I was with one.

But young children in their beauty and innocence insist that their fathers have an emotional life, for how else is a father to know his child, and a child his father? Young children will wail their grief, roar their humor, screech their joy. They relate to their world with perfect immediacy, openness, and clarity. Has anyone ever known a greater passion than that of a six-year-old who believes he has been subjected to an injustice? And a man, if he is to be a father, must *know* his children in these moments of passion; he must *be there* to communicate to his children that it is all right to do things *and* to have feelings about things.

None of us reading the lists of horrors in the daily papers need to be reminded that the consequences of father-failure are drastic. Each week, together with the three other clinicians who comprise the Family Consultation Team, I strive to help families for whom conflict and numbness have occluded the channels of compassionate feeling. We find that in families fueled by anger, the father is frequently either abusive or absent or virtually absent. He is propelled by impulses that snap the ever-more-tenuous fathering bond, and he leaves a child with a space where there should be the image of a loving and honorable man.

When I work in the courts and jails and prisons of our communities I consistently ask my clients—nearly always young men—who comes to mind when I say the word "father," and with equal consistency they offer the same response: a blank stare, a shake of the head, and the monotonous statement "No one." Boys who have not stood beside a loving man for long periods have a way of finding their way into our courts and jails and prisons, where their screams of violence and rage reverberate in the empty fathering space.

This book is lovingly offered in the awareness that many American men have fallen into a terrifying isolation in which individual self-interest has taken precedence over the needs of others, even those others who comprise one's own family. Many men have come to believe, as men have long believed, that our own choices of vocation or role or identity have necessary implications for those around us, and this dependency has contributed to the excessive control of others which has, in turn, marked the first step toward family dissolution.

When this tide of isolation is turned, it will be due to the commitment of millions of individual fathers to the common good. This commitment will take the form of countless small decisions to hold a child, to change a diaper, to patiently offer a finger as a child learns to walk, to be present in the development of the family in a thousand small ways that demonstrate to young life that it is not alone.

Many forces have coalesced to render millions of American children bereft of fathering love. As a nation we are now faced with accepting a future in which fatherlessness is the norm or confronting fathers with a challenge to return to the family and all its stressors, conflicts, and joys. This book offers a modest invitation to the joys that follow when the diverse obligations of fathering love are accepted.

When the agony that accompanies our problems with violence begins to ease it will be because men have chosen to lovingly involve themselves with their children from the very beginning. Far from the media-promulgated image of the deadbeat dad, my wife and I in our fathering workshops again and again discover men who are yearning for this connection, for commitment, and for change. Against all expectation men hold within themselves the potential to do for their own what was never done for them. At some point they show up, they come to learn, these men who would be fathers.

And young children are great teachers; the best teachers because they clearly share the urgency life's lessons hold for them. As we carry them on our shoulders and bounce them on our knees, in another sense we sit at their feet, learning about spontaneity even as we teach them self-control; learning about joy even as we teach them about understanding; learning about love even as we teach them about responsibility.

So these small stories about fathering my two younger sons, Isaac and Aaron, are offered in the large hope that they will help some men enjoy their offspring, as my children have happily invited me to help myself to their joy in being alive. As men are involved with children, that diverse involvement will take the form of countless small stories, each, as with childhood itself, with its own poignant beginning, middle, and end.

As I answered Aaron's profound question with all the awareness of my frailty and love, I knew that my life is larger for having given to him that generous, generative miracle our children ask us to share each day of our lives.

One supplemental note: There is an important reason why none of the following stories describe heartfelt interactions between a father and his daughter. Fate has chosen to grace me with three sons. I believe that most of the meaning of these stories can be generalized to children of both genders; the closeness, warmth, and stunning creativity of children are not monopolized by either sex nor are the challenges to fathers. The message is the same: If fathering love is risked, the daily struggles of life are suffused with joy.

One last note: These stories are arranged for thematic effect. The author begs the reader's understanding regarding any confusion resulting from the children's ages in various stories.

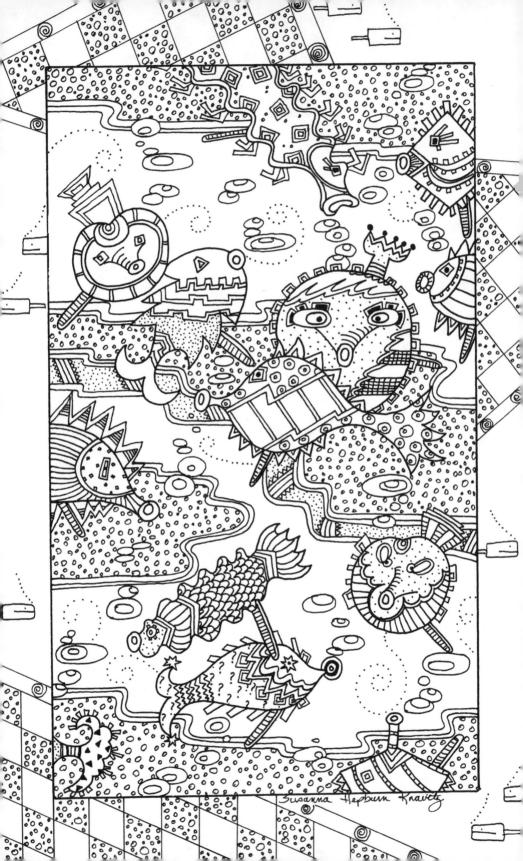

Susanna Hepburn Kravetz

CHAPTER 1
POPSICLE FISH

Slowly the knob turned, and slowly the door was eased open. Four-year-old Aaron's tiny face peeked through the intervening space. I glanced up from my desk.

"Dad," he said haltingly and with a knitted brow. "Are popsicles made of fish?"

Now, this was a question for which I was totally unprepared. To be asked if he could have some ice cream, if he could call up a friend, if he could hit his older brother Isaac in the head with a truck—for all those questions I was ready, but to be asked if popsicles are made of fish, well, the inquiry was so strange it had an Oriental quality, as if he had asked, "Dad, what is the sound of one hand clapping?"

These are the kinds of questions for which children should be paid large sums of money because they stimulate adults' minds to expand more effectively than years of expert psychotherapy. Instinctively, my mind produced an image of a popsicle—a purple one, tall and drippy with two sticks in the bottom—and then an image of a fish—a fat gray trout—and desperately tried to establish a connection between the two.

Alas, no amount of mental strain would induce the popsicle and the fish to consent to belonging together. As a matter of fact, a popsicle and a fish seemed to belong together less than just about any other two things I could imagine. Now, a wrench and an apple, an umbrella and an aardvark, between those I was sure I could in time establish some relationship; but a popsicle and a fish, well, I could not have come up with a more disarming question had I meditated upon it for half a century.

"Well, Aaron," I said at last, falling into my designated adult role as arbiter of common sense. "While it is true that a popsicle is made mostly of water, and a fish swims in water, I can say that if there is one thing about which I feel certain in this world, it is that popsicles are not made of fish."

At this Aaron hesitated for a moment, dropped his head slightly, then turned and ran away, leaving the door ajar behind him. I heard his small feet pounding up the stairs to the room where he was playing with his older brother. "Popsicles are not made of fish! Popsicles are not made of fish!" he shouted as he ran, announcing this information to all like a New Age Paul Revere.

I sat in my study, entranced and wondering, like most parents, if I had "done the right thing." I mean, if a book is made out of a tree, if a blanket is made out of a sheep, if a hot dog is made out of a pig or a chicken or a dog or God knows what else, why not a popsicle made out of a fish? Such a question raises the issue of what is possible and what is not possible, and above all we would like our children to believe that everything is possible. I wondered if I had closed the question off too quickly, jumping to a conclusion and thereby stunting my child's growth and natural curiosity.

The more I thought about it, the more I came to believe that it was not inconceivable that a popsicle could be made out of a fish. I mean, in the day of the nondairy milk shake, why not fish popsicles?

After a few more minutes I was certain I had indeed made a mistake. And what do mature grown-ups do when they err? Well, of course, they admit it to themselves and then they acknowledge their error to those whom they have misinformed.

With a groan I pulled myself erect and plodded upstairs to do my duty. It is not every day that one is faced with the responsibility of acknowledging the possibility of fish popsicles, but when that moment comes, as such moments must in every parent's life, one can only do one's best to face it. Every father must face his comeuppance, as every fish must face his popsicle. Now, it was the time to face mine. I only hoped that when my moment came, I could face my popsicle as gracefully as that fish no doubt faced his.

I found my kids where most parents will find their red-blooded American children on a sunny Saturday afternoon—seated before a computer game, eyes focused hypnotically on the screen.

Now, they were playing computer football, and, having played years of mediocre football in the real world, it was a game to which I was instinctively attracted. In the computer world I could work my way down the field, zigging and zagging, my movements as quick as light itself. In the real world I had been captured from behind by people much stronger than myself and slammed to the ground; in the computer world people, or at least the images that were supposed to stand for people, responded the way they were supposed to.

You can see that I cared deeply about the outcome of the computer football game, no less than I had as I stood on the sidelines of real football games, morose, resenting the hell out of those guys out there wrapping themselves in glory. I always knew that I could do it, but I never did—until I discovered computer football.

So you can imagine my chagrin when I was destroyed thirty-six to two by my six-year-old son Isaac—and I only got the two because he was dancing around as obnoxious guys will when they're winning big. Though I practiced and practiced, I feared he could play with an alacrity that I could never rival—just as I could never compare to those bigger, stronger guys from my younger days.

So it was with a doubled sense of regret that I gingerly lowered myself down to do my duty about the popsicle fish.

"Kids," I said with a suitable air of graveness and responsibility. "Sometimes grown-ups make mistakes too. I mean, just because we're older, should we be expected to be perfect? After all, do we expect you to be perfect?" At this Isaac glanced over at me with opaque eyes. "Well, anyway, about this fish popsicle question, maybe I was a bit overhasty."

Isaac responded, "Oh, Dad," without interrupting his fingers' dance across the keys. "I just sent him down to ask you that so I could play by myself for a while. I know there's no such thing as fish popsicles." At this he shook his head, somehow never removing his eyes from the screen.

I looked at Isaac for a moment. He blithely continued playing. Then I turned to Aaron.

"Hey, Aaron," I said. "Do you know that hot dogs are made out of pigs?"

"Know that," he answered instantly.

"Do you know that paper is made out of a tree?"

"Know that too."

"But do you know that your shirt is made out of a sheep?"

"No."

"Is too."

"Is not."

"Sure it is. If you don't believe me, go ask your mother."

Aaron dropped his computer controller and started hastily down the steps, the words already forming: "Mommy, Mommy, is my shirt made out of a sheep?"

I scooped up the controller and squeezed in beside Isaac. Sometimes there are things a father just has to do.

"But it is possible that popsicles are made of fish, you know," I grumbled as he scored his first touchdown four seconds later. "Anything is possible."

Isaac said, "Sure it is, Dad."

He was generously seeking to spare the sensibilities of a relatively old man who perversely insists on continuing to believe that everything is possible, even fish popsicles.

CHAPTER 2
NUCLEAR BALANCE AND
THE NUCLEAR FAMILY

It was as I was vacuuming the living room that I came to understand how events in Eastern Europe affect us—and how they don't.

Now, I do the vacuuming because, as we all know, men relate better to machines than to people. So, if I can avoid having to relate to my children for forty-five minutes by vacuuming the floor, I consider it a good deal. And besides, I garner a great deal of satisfaction from the approximately seventeen seconds I admire the carpet before it is again covered with torn paper, shards of crayon and clay, and spilled cereal. The clay is particularly troublesome because it congeals onto the fibers of the carpet in such a way that not even the cat can remove it as he shreds the carpet while sharpening his claws.

But back to international politics.

My younger children were solemnly absorbed in the most recent episode of "Teenage Mutant Ninja Turtles" when I decided that the floor needed vacuuming. Or maybe I was vacuuming when the time came for the show. I don't know, but then that's the way these things are; nobody ever knows who started it. The kids couldn't hear the show, so they elevated the volume so that it was much louder than the very loud vacuum.

I yelled at them to turn down the television. I yelled at them louder than the television, which was louder than the very loud vacuum cleaner.

My wife yelled at everyone to come to dinner. She yelled louder than I yelled at the kids to be heard over the television, which was louder than the very loud vacuum cleaner.

The kids then yelled something indiscernible and turned up the television so that they could hear it over my wife's yelling, which needed to be heard over the television, which had been turned up louder than the very loud vacuum cleaner.

You get the picture. Pretty soon the house and everyone in it were ready to explode.

Then I had a brilliant idea. Actually, it was a relatively ordinary idea as ideas go but it's important these days to be self-supportive, so I'll describe it as a brilliant idea.

I turned off the vacuum cleaner. This is known in the parlance as "unilateral de-escalation."

Then my children turned off the television.

We sat down to a (relatively) quiet dinner.

I leaned over and whispered to my wife, "I think I understand what's happening in Eastern Europe."

She nodded wordlessly.

CHAPTER 3
AAAOOOK! THE MADONNA
AND DINOSAUR THOUGHTS

One-and-a-half-year-old Aaron waddles toward the window as I sit watching in the living room chair. It is a sunny morning, and a bright beam of light shines in through the glass, forming a golden rectangle on the carpeted floor. Aaron stops sharply at the edge of the rectangle, teeters for a moment, then reaches out and passes a pudgy hand through the angle of light. His action disturbs the millions of tiny dust motes from their stately procession across the bright ray; the column of light churns in a frenzied, circular swirling.

Aaron smiles. "Aaaoook!" he cries and flaps both hands into the beam of light again and again, calling out in conversation with the curling motes, "Aaaoook! Aaaoook!" His senses are clear and unmuddied, and each happening presents itself with the freshness of a miracle.

Finished with the bright ray, Aaron turns and waddles on, brow intent, the experiential hunter in pursuit of his next prey.

Confirmed member of the "Me Generation" that I am, I sit in my chair thinking about myself. I feel the ennui every dinosaur must have felt as it pondered its own extinction; I know the envy we humanoids know as we witness the sensitive purity of our young.

What happened to me? I wail inwardly, sipping my coffee and scanning my offspring with a shepherd's eye. Now I worry about money, power, the house, money, child care, relationships, and money. Now, if a miracle happened to me, if the Madonna herself appeared to me (I am old enough for the Madonna to have none other than religious associations) and took my hand, I would ask her, robot-like, how I could be of service to her.

But I can remember lying in bed, a little tyke alone in my dark room, anxiously praying for the Madonna *not* to appear. I imagined going downstairs afterward and informing my stolid parents, "I have just had a visitation by the Madonna!" They would be confronted with a choice, either to adjudge me as crazy or believe me, and I had no doubt what the outcome of that choice would be.

For I knew a little girl in our neighborhood who said that she had seen the Madonna in the schoolyard, and she insisted the Madonna would appear again on a certain date. I remember being there that rainy night among the crowd; we milled around, my friends and I, not quite knowing what nine-year-olds say to each other at the scene of a prospective visitation. I never saw the little girl herself but I recall thinking how devout she must be and how deeply her parents must trust her to follow her this far down the path of her devotion.

There were whole families among the crowd, some kneeling over by the schoolyard fence. A TV crew toted cumbersome equipment, shining a bright light here and there into a surprised face. I noticed that those who kneeled tended to kneel together and those who held themselves apart were grouped farther out on the black expanse of pavement. I wondered if this was how God divided the sinners and the saved. Were choices of terrible significance being made here?

Small and shut off from the main scene, I stared at a grown-up's back as the appointed hour approached. The buzz increased and for a moment I believed that the Madonna had in fact appeared as planned, as hoped, that she was standing there, somewhere in the vast land beyond this man's sleeve, shining, arms extended, welcoming all who believed to share in the joy of her pure light.

But empty time went on; nothing happened. The crowd grew restive. Eventually, the TV crew rolled up its cords and we all started toward home, and as I walked I remember thinking of that little girl, now sad in her shame, her parents no doubt still supporting her, the three of them united but now against a disbelieving world.

So as I lay in my bed alone in the dark I fervently prayed to be spared an apparition; if the Madonna had appeared I would have begged her to keep this just between the two of us, a personal thing, and that if she ever appeared to me in company I hoped she would not be too insulted if I ignored her. For it was not that I lacked faith, it was just that the mantle of fame was far too wide for my small shoulders, and I had hard work to do in this world yet.

These are the thoughts that dinosaurs think as they witness the magic of their young. As Aaron turns and races onto my lap and I squeeze his perfect tiny body in my arms, I realize that those moments, those moments years before and ten thousand times since, when self-protection was fearfully chosen over the wild release of affirmation, are the barriers that separate us, each from the other. I know in my dinosaur mind that in time my beautiful son will leave his shining world behind and will join me on my dusty shelf; and there we will sit for a moment together on high, thinking as one deep dinosaur thoughts, living as one our brief dinosaur time.

CHAPTER 4
NO EASY DECISIONS

The countless daily decisions parents make concerning their children are so complex, and so important, it is amazing anything ever gets done at all.

Just the other morning I sent Isaac and Aaron on ahead of me to the car as I rushed around jamming cereal boxes into cabinets and tossing dirty dishes in the sink before driving them to school and myself to work. For three, maybe four minutes, they were alone. That, of course, was an opening for mayhem.

I jumped into the car to discover a look of concern and guilt, respectively, on the two boys' faces. The six-year-old, being the subject of the mayhem, was the one who disclosed it.

"Isaac burned a hole in my coat with the lighter," Aaron said, describing the latest incident as if reporting the morning's weather. He twisted around and displayed a small circular black mark on the front of his parka. From it emanated a vague acrid stench of burned plastic.

So. The deed had been done. One heavily scented black mark on coat, allegedly caused by contact with auto cigarette lighter. Alleged perpetrator: Isaac, age eight. Those were the facts. As is usually the case with life, it is after the facts are established that things get complicated.

Isaac insisted he had merely been testing the lighter, conducting a routine experiment in the thermal properties of metal, when Aaron turned toward him and thrust his body atop the lighter. Isaac struggled heroically to spare him from injury. Alas, this one small but visible mark was the sad but inevitable consequence of Aaron's youthful impulsiveness.

Each day, from six to 1,097 times, a parent faces such moments of decision. Who is to blame? What direction will the conversation take from here? Should I accept Isaac's version at face value and chastise Aaron for his accursed squirminess? Should I take both of their coats and make them walk to school exposed to the hostile elements? How can I determine who is telling the truth in the six minutes before I must appear at work?

As I sat contemplating these familiar dilemmas, a vision entered my mind. I saw Isaac pushing in and then withdrawing the lighter. Armed with this small, brilliant sword, he felt like a character from *Star Wars*—he was a hero in search of an opponent. With whom to do battle? With his brother, of course, no other more despised entity being readily available. A few wavings of the swo— I mean, lighter—a brief parry by Aaron, another thrust to the midsection, and, touché! The very satisfying but forbidden burn mark was applied.

This vision came to me with the verisimilitude of certain truth. It perfectly fit both characters and the situation. So, though I had no concrete evidence to support my version, I accepted it as reality. The kids would just have to live with it.

Isaac was guilty. Case closed.

Now for the sentencing, the execution of which could take no more than the four and one-half minutes that remained. A lecture always does nicely in these situations since the length can be altered to fit and the volume moderated or increased to compensate for brevity of time.

So I yelled at Isaac for a while about responsibility, about maturity, about caring for others, about brushing his teeth, about putting his socks in the hamper, and suchlike. I even used the old "How would you feel if someone did that to you?" routine, which usually is good for a few moments of guilt.

In order to understand how you would feel if something that was done to someone else was done unto you, you must first have

developed what the Swiss psychologist Piaget called "reversibility":
the ability to turn things around in your mind and honestly imagine
what life would be like if things were the reverse of what they are.
Piaget hypothesized that children develop this capacity somewhere
between the ages of five and ninety-five and that it is an essential
aspect of the process of socialization.

Whether Isaac could engage in this reversal or not, he appeared
suitably forlorn for about five seconds. Then his attention shifted to a
much more important difficulty.

He was afraid that Aaron, with his big mouth, would blab to
everyone at the school about what he had done. If Aaron had his way,
everyone, all the boys and all the girls, and not just the girls he hated
but even the one girl he thought was really pretty, would know that
Isaac was a jacket burner. This was a serious problem.

Aaron, of course, seized his moment of power and assured Isaac
that he would indeed tell everybody, most particularly that special
someone. Yes, they would know, they would all know in detail that
Isaac was an unrecovered jacket burner, and he himself would display
the evidence. Touché.

Isaac turned to me with a pleading look.

Decision #2: Whether to utilize parental power to prevent Aaron
from blabbing to everyone about Isaac's troublesome history. Is there
a larger issue here regarding family honor?

Naah. Decision #2, really just an extension of decision #1,
involves leaving Isaac with the terrible uncertainty of not knowing
whether his brother will blab. All day long his little brother will walk
tall, elevated by his secret power. Such are the natural consequences
with which jacket burners must live.

As they got out of the car, I kissed Isaac with a bit more gravity
than usual, meanwhile prying a bit of sleep from the corner of his
eye. It's a tough life, kid, I wanted to say, and we all have our
regrets. But when you play with fire, sometimes you get burned—and
sometimes somebody else does. If it happens, you've just got to live
with it.

Just as every parent must live with the terrible uncertainty of not knowing whether those thousand crucial decisions were the right ones.

CHAPTER 5
BIG BOYS DO CRY

J ust the other day Aaron Malachi came out with a question that captures the unfortunate essence of what it means to be a man in America.

He was sitting—well, actually, squirming—on the edge of the kitchen counter while we engaged in one of our frequent ticklefests. Ticklefests are frequent because Aaron's laughter is so guttural, so free and unrestrained, that it is a joy to hear. A seven-year-old may struggle to keep a straight face as grown-up fingers poke at armpits and pectorals, but a five-year-old is still young and un-self-conscious enough to completely abandon both body and mind to the explosive release of laughter.

Though most grown-ups detest it, daily tickling would probably greatly benefit our health. Research has shown that frequent laughter improves the functioning of the immune system; Norman Cousins in his well-known book *Anatomy of an Illness* describes how he shook off an immunological disorder by subjecting himself to repeated showings of Laurel and Hardy and Abbott and Costello movies. The laughing cure, it's called.

But during our recent ticklefest Aaron pulled himself away and his face assumed a serious cast. He raised a small hand to my cheek.

"Daddy," he said, knitting his brow, "do you ever cry? Did you ever cry when you were little?"

I was taken aback. Of course I can cry, I felt like responding. I can walk, I can talk, I can work, I can drive a car, and I can cry.

But the truth of the matter is that I do walk, talk, work, and drive—but I don't cry. I suppose I could, and I can vaguely remember when I last did, but saying that I do cry is akin to saying that I can throw a discus eighty yards because I did it once on a summer afternoon twenty-five years ago.

"You never cried even once while I was alive," Aaron persisted. And he was right. In all the years he had been on the planet, tears had never crossed my cheeks. I did get a little choked up in the birthing room as I watched him emerge into the world—but, what with all the nurses and all, I restrained myself.

No, Aaron had never seen me cry—he'd seen me laugh, seen me silent, and he'd seen me angry. Oh, yes, he'd seen me angry lots of times.

For that's what men do—men get angry. They don't get sad, they get even, or they try to, anyway, and they usually end up farther behind than ever. The fact that the average man dies about seven years earlier than the average woman has stimulated research into the reasons for this discrepancy, resulting in the widespread belief that "Type A" personalities—hard-driving, ambitious achiever types—are at considerably increased risk of heart disease and early death. But recent studies indicate it is not Type A behavior that is the culprit but rather anger, frequent, misdirected, festering anger, which slowly wears down men and ultimately kills them.

The big hypothesis is that men get angry because they are afraid to be sad, to cry. Testosterone and social conditioning may play a role, but the man in the midst of a furious tirade is also afraid to say, honestly and forthrightly, that his feelings have been hurt. Anger is easier, less risky. Anger is the modern male addiction, and like most addictions, in time it is fatal.

It is not purely coincidental that Aaron should ask me about crying while in the midst of a bout of laughter. Laughter and weeping are intimately related and may even be slightly different forms of the same emotional release.

Many years ago, a few days after graduating from college, I was sitting around with some classmates cracking jokes before we said farewell to each other and took our separate directions in life. Suddenly, after a friend made a particularly riotous comment, my tears of hysterical laughter transformed ever so imperceptibly into tears of grief—sobbing, gut-wrenching grief.

The grief was well deserved, I can see now. I was leaving behind friends, a home, a community of which I would never again be a part. But even though I was among friends who would have understood and even shared my sadness, I was embarrassed, and I stifled my grief out of shame at my tears.

And, now that I think about it, that may have been the last time I cried—quite a few years, as Aaron said, before he was alive. I wonder how this has affected Aaron, what he has learned from seeing me funny, seeing me angry, but never once seeing me wholly, truly sad. Maybe it means that he too will forget how to cry. Or maybe it means that I will know him seven years less than I would have, had I had access to my tears.

That part really makes me sad. Not angry, no. Sad.

CHAPTER 6
BUNGEE SMILE

I was driving through the center of town when I noticed the little girl. She had short, brown hair and a dark complexion contrasting with the brilliance of her eyes. She looked to be about five years old. She was standing in a paved parking area just off the curbstone, head leaned back as she gazed upward at an adult who stood before the open door of a late model gray Pontiac. Behind her Christmas lights blinked on and off in a store window, illuminating the surrounding sidewalk in a multichromatic haze.

It was pure coincidence that my eyes saw her as she stood small beside the front fender of the car. Then, as I watched, her face lit up with a wide smile of unmitigated joy. She leaned back, her small dark eyes locked on the adult holding the car door, her face compressed with laughter, the smile stretching ever more widely across her face and her eyes disappearing in a maze of wrinkles.

Meanwhile, as usual, Isaac and Aaron were in the backseat, arguing.

"A person could too jump off a bridge that was four hundred feet high with a bungee cord tied to his leg!" shouted Aaron.

"Could not!" said Isaac in a tone damp with condescension. "A cord that long would break and splat! The person would be dead."

"Could so! What if he jumped out of an airplane?"

"What's he going to do, drag behind the airplane ten thousand feet up in the air? You're such an idiot."

"Daaaad!" shouted Aaron. "Couldn't someone jump off a cliff

from forty feet with a bungee cord tied to his leg?"

"Forty feet!" Isaac leapt in. "You said four hundred! Four hundred! Don't you know the difference between forty and four hundred?"

"I said forty *stories*!"

"*Hundred!*"

"Did not!"

"Did so!"

"Not!"

"So!"

"Not!"

"So!"

"Notnotnotnotnotnotnotnotnot!"

"Sososososososososo!"

The little girl was still grinning hugely as I left her behind. I turned my head a bit to prolong the moment, such pure joy, this momentary interaction between a child and a person who cares for her.

"The key thing is," I said over my shoulder toward Aaron, "how long a bungee cord you talking about?"

"Oh, like forty stories," he said, "forty or sixty."

"That's more than four hundred feet," I said. "That's a mighty long bungee cord."

"See?" said Isaac, waving his mittened hand in front of his younger sibling's face. "You are an idiot!"

"What if he was wearing a parachute?" Aaron insisted, knocking the hand aside, "Or two parachutes?"

"Why would he wear a parachute if he had a bungee cord?" asked Isaac. I could see him rolling his eyes in frustration.

The dark road wove through the hills, old overhanging trees blotting out the street lamps. A brightly lit store emerged from the unbroken line of the forest, lent its brilliant cacophony to the road for a moment, then receded into the darkness behind. I wondered if the little girl was still smiling, how long she smiled before she climbed into the car and relaxed into her seat, perhaps falling asleep in the warm car on the long ride home. In that moment, she was probably as happy as she would ever be in her life, and her sleep would be undisturbed by any thought of her loss.

That's the way it is with happiness, I thought, it's only by forgetting about it that we really have it.

And that's why the happiness of children is so perfect and so pure. It's not yet complicated by the grown-up anticipation of its ending, which infests all happiness with a distance and a worry that makes it not-quite-happiness and leaves the subject irrevocably in the somber world of adults.

That's the way it is. Each time you jump off the bridge the bungee cord brings you back safely, so you stretch it out more and more and more until one time you stretch it so far it snaps—and of course until that time, until that very moment, you had no idea that it ever could break; you assumed that the cord was one of those certain facts of life like life and death and taxes—and then, in a moment, you're on your own. You can't ever find your way back to that perfect, unmitigated joy that knows no beginning or ending and you have to start making do with what is, with what you've got, and that's the burdensome awareness of big-brained creatures of the extension of things, of their startings and stoppings, and from that moment on the bungee cord has snapped and you won't laugh like that little girl anymore.

"Dad, wouldn't a parachute save you if you jumped off a forty-story building?" Aaron shouted. "Wouldn't it save you? Wouldn't it? Wouldn't it?"

"Sure," I said, "as long as you opened it right away."

"What would your bungee cord do then?" Isaac jumped in, "Leave you hanging upside down in your parachute. Maybe you'd get tangled up and die." This part was uttered with a note of hopefulness.

"Would not!" the Aaron said.

"Would so!"

"Not!"

"So!"

The dark road twisted around a curve and over a small hill. A convenience store emerged from the darkness on the right, shone brilliantly, dropped away into the dark.

Again I thought of the little girl and her smile and the great bungee cord of life.

"Tell you what," I said. "Next place we see, we'll stop for something to eat."

"I'll bet it'll be in ten thousand miles," said Aaron, pouting.

I glanced in the rearview mirror in time to see the Isaac cover his eyes with his mittens. "Dad," he said, his words muffled by the thick wool of his gloves. "He's driving me crazy."

"Just hang on, both of you," I answered. "Wherever it is, we'll get there soon enough."

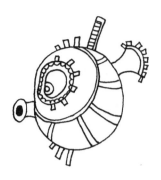

CHAPTER 7
LOVE, SWEET LOVE

I admit it with shame but it's true. When you do things that are hurtful to other people, even those whom you love, it's not easy to come clean, to let the cat out of the bag. There's a tendency to do things on the sly, behind people's backs, to slink around, glancing over your shoulder at every turn. Finally, when you just can't stand it anymore, when the deception and the guilt are overwhelming, you've just got to put your cards on the table, no matter how sorry a hand you may be holding. And now it's my time to make a clean breast of it.

I buy candy for my small children. Now and then—all too often, I know—on the way home from work I'll stop at a convenience store and purchase two big chunks of chocolate, one for each child. Shortly after I come in the door, they race up to give me my hello hugs—they're no fools—and I cast a furtive glance to the right and left and slip them the candy. Having made their score, they disappear into some far corner of the house where they sit alone, cheeks bulging and minds racing with chocolate.

You see, my wife is a whole-grain person, the kind of person who drinks spinach juice mixed with mangled garlic. With her determining our diet my oldest son never lost his baby teeth, and he would still have them now as he packs for the Coast Guard had I not paid some dentist hundreds to pull them, still spotless, from his head.

Now, back when I was a kid, back before Mohawks or Bo Jackson, back when Madonna referred to a blessed personage, I would leave school with change jangling in my pocket and then would leave the candy store with a big bag of malted milk balls, which I would pop into my mouth one at a time and continuously until they were all gone—all fifty of them. I could feel the sugars racing to the surface of my skin. I could feel the pores open and a light sweat would appear on my brow. My eyes would become glassy with the dullness of the sated chocolate addict. When I was seven, the dentist had to chip out the stumps of my teeth with a pick. Those were the days.

But those days are gone. Now, with their morning chewable vitamins, vitamin-fortified granola, and vitamin-fortified milk, my kids get more nutrition before seven-thirty than I got before my first date—and I skipped the junior and senior proms. And for lunch, at school my kids have salad with real green lettuce and red tomatoes, vegetables crisp with life. Why, back in my day, back before John Cougar became John Cougar Mellencamp, back before John Mellencamp became John Cougar again, back before the Grateful Dead were born, a can of spaghetti was good food, and school lunches had vegetables with the consistency of a mud slide and nearly as pleasant a flavor. We knew those vegetables had never, ever seen the light of day, that they were made in a dark factory somewhere by huge, angry men operating colossal iron shovels. Whereas my sons' crisp vegetables are consumed with a crunch, our vegetables hit our plates with a splat. Ah, those were the days.

Now, I must confess, when I bring my youngest son along on some weekend errand I'll stop at a roadside store and pick him up a bag of candy. There he'll sit, quiet on the seat beside me, his tiny fingers rummaging down into the bag for the last M&M, popping it into his mouth as he gazes entranced out the windshield. I am pleased to know that now, for at least thirty seconds, he is happy, as purely, unambivalently happy, as he will ever be in his life.

I know it's wrong to make kids happy with candy, bad for their teeth in the short run, maybe bad for their soul in the long, but then I think about global warming and the national debt and the savings and loan crisis and nuclear proliferation and toxic wastes and the deterioration of our educational system and other pleasantries he's going to have to deal with when he grows up and I think, what the hell. I turn to him where he sits small in the seat and I say:

"Hey, little guy. How about a milk shake to go with that twenty-four-ounce chunk of chocolate?"

And as he turns his glassy, sated gaze upon me his eyes are filled with—well, it's not love, I know, but for once he's sure I understand. Maturity and wisdom may someday fail, but we will remember when candy brought us together one more time.

CHAPTER 8
THE DONUTS OF THE MIND

While my wife slept in, the three of us were on a Sunday morning donut run. Aaron and Isaac picked out a bunch of chocolate-covered, cream-filled donuts. I ordered a few more just to make sure there would be enough left over for me. Then, with the two boys battling over the donut box, we were on our way.

On the way home, to give my wife a few extra minutes of blissful silence, I pulled down a side street leading to the Natural Bridge State Park in North Adams, Massachusetts. Since it was early on a midwinter Sunday morning, the place was deserted. We snuck under the restraining wire and began exploring the place.

For those who have not had the pleasure of visiting Natural Bridge State Park, it consists of a carefully fenced path that runs among steep stone ravines, at the faraway bottom of which rush torrents of wild water.

Aaron had a hard time walking to the thin edge of the overlook, far above the roaring river. The primeval stone walls looked damp and hard. The water was cold and very, very far down. I think he could clearly imagine how his small body would feel should he somehow tumble over that fence and hurtle down, down into that cold water.

It made me remember a story from my traveling days. I was trudging up a dark tower in Florence, Italy. When the group I was accompanying finally got to the top someone pushed open a door. We walked out onto a sunny platform far above the city square. There were no fences, no railings, just an open deck from which we could spy tiny antlike beings far below.

It was one of those situations where you hoped so fervently not to get dizzy that it made you dizzy. It was a situation in which you devote a lot of mental effort to making sure that you don't suddenly suffer from the delusion that you are the one human being who can fly. The view was great, but I didn't much care about that. A human being's capacity to remain erect is directly proportional to his distance from the ground.

Or maybe my six-year-old son's hesitancy was related to something else. Those huge ravines, surrounded by dark rock, looked mighty mysterious on that bleak midwinter morning. There was something strange about them, something deep and strange.

It reminded me that the mind is deep and strange, that there are things going on in it, things we don't know or understand, all the time.

To use an innocuous example: If you, like many people, played the piano for a year when you were a kid before your parents finally let you quit, you may have had the experience of sitting down at the pearly whites fifteen years later and realizing that, if you just let your fingers go, they will perform precisely as they did in the dim and distant past. It's as if your fingers recall what your conscious memory has forgotten. It's all still there, somewhere, percolating around in the mixture that is you.

There are those medical scientists who would have us believe that the mind is limited to the brain and that all of our experiences are merely a matter of chemical events occurring at nerve endings. But I will have none of it. I believe that, decades or centuries hence, when we finally begin to have some understanding of these things, we will discover that it is all a lot more complex, and at the same time a lot more simple, than that.

Years ago, I was involved in a collision between a motorcycle and a truck. Unfortunately, I was driving the motorcycle. I lay in the hospital for six days, doing funny things like mixing the chocolate pudding and the mashed potatoes and then putting the concoction between slices of bread. I did these things, but I was not there.

On the sixth day, for reasons completely unknown to me but that would be all-too-simply explained by a neurologist, I had a dream that my high school wrestling coach was kneeling beside the mat during the regional championships. He was screaming at me as I struggled beneath my opponent.

"Get up, Murphy, get up!" he shouted. "No one can hold you! Get up!"

I got up. I found myself in a hospital bed. I was gazing at the guy in the next bed, who had just had a leg removed due to cancer. I was back.

I left the hospital the next day, thrilled with the joy of those who have just experienced something truly mysterious and uncertain, but have been spared its most awful consequences. I'm not sure what I thought before all this, but since that moment I have not been able to believe that we understand a hell of a lot about the human mind. Looking down into that particular ravine has helped me to remain modest and at least a little realistic.

With some coaxing my six-year-old son held my hand and together we approached the edge of the walkway and gazed way, way down into the distant spiral of rushing water.

Yep, it sure was a long way down. It was thrilling, and a little scary, but, you know how it is, we couldn't help but look. That's another one of those things about the mind that doesn't have too much to do with brain chemistry.

And the chocolate donuts, they were great, too.

Susanna Hepburn Kravitz

CHAPTER 9
THE GREAT BIG EXPLOSION
CALLED LIFE

Three of us were crammed into the front of the pickup truck as I drove my adolescent son to his after-school job. Ben had the window seat. Aaron was in the middle, snuggled under my elbow.

It's nice having a little kid tucked under your arm, with your elbow gently massaging his tiny nose at every hard right-hand turn. They fit in under there and they sit like they belong there, relaxed and perceiving the world from their safe place.

When we got to the hamburger stand without the golden arches Ben hopped out with a quick good-bye and I pulled away.

Then to my surprise Aaron abandoned his position beneath my elbow, hiked himself across the seat, and buckled himself in beside the window.

"What're you doin'?" I asked.

"I like it over here by the window," he replied.

Hhmmph. Time passes. It doesn't wait for anybody. It just scoots right on by, like my son scooting across the seat to the window.

Families are kind of like the universe, which according to reliable sources in the beginning was an incredibly dense, intimate, heavy little ball that then blew up and has been flying apart ever since.

Mothers nurture a tiny developing life inside them for a long time and then deliver a baby, and the baby starts moving away, never to return.

A father cares for his children, holds them, teaches them as best he can, fights with them, positions himself between them and a crazy, dangerous, beautiful world. Then one day the son comes home and says, "Hey, Mom and Dad, I'm going to Cincinnati. I'll see you later." And that's it.

From about zero to six years old it's as if the kid's body belongs to you. You can hold 'em, pick 'em up and carry 'em around, schmush their faces and rub noses and pull on their incredibly perfect little toes, clap their tiny hands together and pass your palm, ever so gently, over a hard, rounded, finely haired forehead. You can feel the life beneath your hand; you can feel the perfect, pure, brilliant, unmuddied brain still flawlessly connected to everything else, still sensing with unviolated openness your hand, the world, yourself.

But then, somewhere around six or eight or so, they start to decide that their body is their own. They start to pull away when you want to rub noses or blow farts on their neck. They don't laugh with that absolute and total abandon anymore but instead they push their hands against your chest and say, with some irritation, "Daaadeee!"

And then you know the planets are really moving away, the universe is exploding pretty damn fast now, and it's time to get out the binoculars and then the telescope and finally, just a few seconds hence, the old discolored picture books that show how they looked when their legs were chubby and bowed and their cheeks were as round as a couple of crab apples but about a million times as soft.

Just last week I went to visit my father in the Old Soldier's Home. For a few hours I watched him, an Alzheimer's victim, struggling to remember a name, a place, an event. He substituted relationship statements like "Well, you've just got to have the right tool for the job" or "He was a guy who would get it done." As for all the specific information, including my name and all the individual biographical data about me, it was gone from the memory of my father forever.

As I left a while later, I pictured him standing at the window of his room, looking out over the parking lot as his wife and son walked out beyond the hospital walls that now defined the boundaries of his world. Over and over the same phrase came to my mind, "It's just so much life!" The pain and turmoil and disappointments of family life seemed insignificant, even as did the joys. It was just that it happened—so much life, so much life! I mean, deterioration and death are inevitable and must be accepted, as must life, but somehow it is the individual circumstances that are missed, the nose rubbings, the arm wrestlings, the Sunday dinners and the Monday mornings in crowded bathrooms—the million tiny moments of sharing that comprise a family.

So much life, when viewed from the end, so much passion and time and daily drama, all fading into the past, all moving away into some other universe as the power of the explosion of creation peters out and disappears.

I can imagine each one of us, eventually, drifting out there on the edge of the universe and gaping wide-eyed and slack-faced out at God knows what, wanting only in some center part of ourselves to go home again, to sit at the kitchen table of our childhood and stare out a window, to schmush a few noses and hug a few small, perfect bodies, to radiate the love and compassion and terrible, terrible urgency we feel as we realize that it is all moving away, no matter how much we want to hold onto it, it is all moving away, and all we can do is remember to wave good-bye.

So, I reached over and scruffled the hair on Aaron's head—he wanted that spike so much I had to give in, even in this weird age when I beg my kids to grow their hair long—and he kept on gazing out the window at the passing world.

"So hey, kid, how 'bout we go get an ice cream cone?" I suggested.

"Naahh," he said, without taking his eyes off the view. "I'm not hungry for ice cream."

There he goes, I thought. Growing up and away for his own ride on that great big explosion called life.

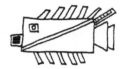

CHAPTER 10
GROWING UP YOUNG

The topic of this morning's breakfast meeting between four-year-old Aaron and his brother Isaac is the time-honored question: What are you going to be when you grow up?

Between mouthfuls of cereal Aaron volunteers that he wants to be a soldier; all the blamming! and the banging! suit his interests just fine—and throw in an extra large BOOM! while you're at it.

Isaac, reasoned and sagacious at six, can think the consequences of these choices through: "But if you are a soldier, you could be killed by your *emeny*," he says, giving his error particular emphasis. "Or you could have to find and kill your *emeny*."

Finishing his cereal Isaac picks up his crayons and begins coloring. "Me, I'm going to be an artist," he says pensively. Then he turns to me: "Daddy, when I get older, remind me not to be a soldier, okay?"

Without reluctance I assure him that I will remind him not to be a soldier—in fact, after spending $250,000 on his education, I will physically prevent him from becoming a soldier.

But Aaron can no longer contain his excitement at the imminent prospects of soldierdom: "Mommy doesn't want me to be a soldier," he says, hands gesticulating, "but if the bad turtles came and tried to get Mommy, I'd just BLAM!" His cheeks are florid with the vision of bad turtles hurtling about the rooms of his imagination. "They'd be cryin'!" he says in conclusion. The bad turtles are repulsed. Mommy is saved. Indeed, he who messes with the mother of a four-year-old is in deep, deep trouble.

The six-year-old, more experienced in the ways of pain and hurt, will stand, serious and stolid, guarding the gate to home and Mommy. The four-year-old, as yet heedless of fearsome consequences, can think of nothing better than to swing screaming down from a rope to kick the invader in the teeth. Four-year-olds are the point children in the army of youth, forever crashing through doors or down stairs, suddenly appearing with a thud! or a bang! Six-year-olds, conversely, take a more balanced view; anticipating potential catastrophe as well as victory, they move with caution and care.

Indeed, in their play Isaac is invariably "the Captain" and Aaron "the Commander"—captain outranks commander in their imaginary world—so Aaron is the one designated to hurl his small body down a grassy hill or into the middle of a mud puddle.

Therefore, four-year-olds end up crying more often—at least until they promote themselves to captain.

I know this to be true because I've done field research with live subjects; true, there was a population in the study of only two, and all the subjects were male, but I know from personal experience that dissertations have been published with less. Still I wonder whether these are enduring character traits or mere age-related stuff, whether Aaron will end up a stunt car driver or deep sea-diver and Isaac a stockbroker or dentist or, by chance, a psychologist.

Meanwhile, Isaac and Aaron have switched their attention to toy cars. Isaac has of course allocated himself a fearsome-looking bulldozer and Aaron a rather battered-looking Ford Escort.

They smash the cars together in a series of frontal assaults and inevitably Aaron bangs his hand, bringing on tears. As I comfort him I realize that, all this philosophizing aside, someday he really will grow up. This thought fills me with terror and grief; I give him an extra hug for all the times when he is big and is a real artist or soldier or stunt car driver and such gestures will be passé or geographically impossible.

When he squirms free a moment later Aaron smiles and laughs and fetches me a fearsome wallop to the shoulder, then, with a loud

"Hieeeyaah!" a karate kick to the shin.

I pray for my body's sake that all this will change as he grows up and finds his way, but in this, as in so many other things, only time will be the teacher.

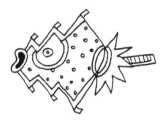

CHAPTER 11
HOMESICK AND WELL

The statement came out of the cold blue of a February morning. Aaron stood beside the kitchen table, shoveling Shredded Wheats into his mouth; one of the many good things about being four years old is that tables are at just the right height for standing while eating—and as every parent knows, four-year-olds don't like to sit down.

"I'm homesick!" Aaron exclaimed.

I was mystified. "But Aaron, you've never been away from home in your life! How could you be homesick?"

Aaron's sagacious six-year-old brother Isaac elaborated, as he is wont to do, from where he sat across the table. "It's like when you're bored," he explained patiently. "He means that he's bored of home."

That started me thinking about what home is like for kids. Most grown-ups don't remember the way the world looked when we were three-odd feet shorter than we are today. At the crawling age, coffee tables are at head height, but if you duck you can get under them quite easily. And quite interesting things may be found there: pieces of toys, tasty chunks of old food, dust balls—the slim area between the back of the couch and the wall is a regular gold mine of home artifacts, as any grown-up who has finally decided to do a thorough cleaning has discovered.

It's revealing to observe a crawler at the top of the stairs, as he peeks over the edge, then carefully turns his body around before

clambering down backward. My personal definition of the end of
infancy is when a child finally decides to descend the stairs facing
forward. By extension, the end of toddlerhood is when a child begins
"stepping over" as he comes down the stairs rather than placing both
feet on each step as he descends. When that happens, it's time to start
saving for college.

They say that crawling is good for the development of intelligence
and mental balance. Most yoga courses prescribe a five-minute period
of crawling as a daily exercise, although most of us fulfill our
minimum daily crawling requirement as we leave the bosses' office
each day.

For young children, though, the world of grown-ups consists of
knees and thighs and hips. Kids notice belt buckles. The faces and
heads of grown-ups exist in a far-distant land, like the peaks of
mountains. On certain ancient peaks, snow remains all the year round.

Kids notice the feel and look of things: the sheen on a brass
doorknob, right at eye level, the rough feel of carpeting on the palm
of the hand. Kids love to pile up cushions and make cozy spaces, the
better to replicate the warm security of the womb. Then, having
gotten bored, they are reborn, bursting out and beating each other
over the head with the cushions, stopping only when they knock over
a lamp.

As I descend the stairs behind my children, I notice something else
about kids: They slow you down. To go for a walk with a small child,
and to allow him to determine the pace, is to enter a different
temporal dimension, to possess a wealth of time beyond telling. He
stoops to pick up every stick or stone and cast it into a stream,
transfixed by the small splash it makes. Stone after stone he throws:
throwing, watching, throwing, watching.

Either you slow down and get into it or you get impatient and drag
him on before he's ready. He hands you stones to carry until your
pockets are stuffed with lumpy weights, stones he will line up on his
bureau top that evening before bed, reminding you that you at least
accomplished something useful that day: You collected stones, stones

you'll discover as you clean out a back closet twenty years hence, and then, too, they will cause you to stop, your eyes will glaze over for a moment, and you will remember.

You'll remember a time when your kids taught you about time and home, about a time when there was time enough to be "homesick," about a time when each curtain, cushion, and doorknob had the magical meaning of home.

And now, as Aaron stuffs the final Shredded Wheat into his small mouth, I ask him one final question: "Well, if you're so homesick, where would you rather be right now?"

He straightens up and says through a mouthful, "Oh, the Bahamas!"

And sometimes, when they feel at home, small children speak the thoughts of the adults who love them.

CHAPTER 12
WITHOUT STRINGS

This very Sunday morning my eleven-year-old son put his own dollar into the collection plate. Thirty seconds later his younger brother yanked on my sleeve and, his voice lowered out of respect for the religious setting, whispered, "Isaac just called me a pig!"

I leaned over to Isaac, who I knew was bragging about his generosity, and hissed in his ear that I had a story to tell him. Then on the way home I quoted that line from Scripture—the one that says when you're being charitable your left hand shouldn't know what your right hand is doing.

"Of course, if you're left-handed," I said to my nine-year-old son, who is a southpaw, "then I guess you shouldn't let your right hand know what your left hand is doing."

Aaron, the nine-year-old, stared at his hands and looked confused. "But I bat right-handed."

"Well, that's a problem," I answered. "Then you can't let your hands talk to each other at all."

"He'll have to give with both hands tied behind his back," chimed in Isaac. He continued in a more somber tone. "But I know what you mean. It means that when you're generous you should shut up about it."

"Now, why do you think that is?" I asked, aping the ancient dialogical method.

Aaron picked up on it, perhaps because as the younger brother he needs to prove himself. Or maybe he has some kind of natural gift for interpretation. Last night I spent half an hour struggling to unscramble a word in a newspaper puzzle. I tried "ruslaw" and "lawsur" and "slawru." Finally Aaron came to the table and peered over my shoulder. Three seconds later he said, "How about walrus?"

It's a staggering moment when a child demonstrates talents beyond those of his parents. You want it to happen, you want your children to strike off into lands you never explored, but then there's a wound, a deep loss as old as humanity itself. It means that the best thing you can do for your children is to get out of their way.

"If you make a big deal out of giving something, out of being generous," Aaron said, moving his now-communicating hands in the air between us, "then it means you're trying to get something out of it, you're trying to get credit, which means you're not being so generous."

"It's more like a trade," Isaac added, not wanting to see his brother get too far out in front. "When you want credit for doing something good it's like a business deal. You give away something, but you make sure you're getting something in return."

This difference between trading and giving was made clear to me by a social worker friend who took me to lunch. As we walked down the street afterward, I told him how much I had enjoyed it and that I wanted to return the favor soon.

My friend stopped and turned toward me. "Listen," he said intensely. "I took you to lunch because I wanted to. It's a gift! You don't have to give anything back!"

He was right. I had offered to take him to lunch because I hated being indebted to him or to anyone. I wanted to make sure he didn't have anything on me. I was so used to emotional trading that whenever I received anything from anyone, I assumed the debt would soon come due. It was the uncertainty of not knowing what would be asked in return that involved a loss of control I couldn't tolerate. I had to clear it up, make explicit the terms of the deal right away.

That is the way a man has to be, I thought. The ideal position of masculine strength was to give and receive nothing. Giving and receiving nothing, you keep what you've earned and never run up any debts. If the worst happened, you could always walk away, free and clear. In a business deal or in a family you have to remain on top, and the only way to make sure you remain on top is to trust no one.

So on those rare occasions when someone does give you something, gives it cleanly and without expectation of return, you eye them suspiciously and mutter, "Hey, no thanks. I'm okay just the way I am."

But, of course, we are not okay the way we are. We spend eight quadzillion nights alone in rooms wondering if life was meant to be this way, staring at the walls at three in the morning and wondering what went wrong. Was it that we were too selfish, too selfish to accept a pure gift? And have we thereby neglected a moment of opportunity that will never come again?

It's a lesson most of us men never learn, the difference between giving and trading. We stand tall on our long legs, thinking, planning, expecting. We trade at work and we trade at home, and then we wonder why the deals at home are so much more complicated, and why we don't get any feeling of satisfaction even when we think we've won.

It's hard for a man to tell the difference between giving, trading, and receiving; it's hard, but it's important. It's important because if we fail to comprehend the difference we may as well be dead or even never have lived. There is something deep inside us that wants to put a dollar in the collection plate with absolute purity, so that even the big brain that sits lordly between the two hands doesn't know what we have done. And the child who knows that this is how honor comes into the world will take the torch of humanity from us and carry it where he will.

We arrived at the fast-food restaurant where, each week, we have breakfast after church. We stood silent in the reception area, the three of us clad incongruously in our Sunday best. While we waited, to my surprise, Isaac came to me and offered to pay for the meal with some of his Christmas money.

That'll be about fifteen bucks, I thought. I felt safe, I have to admit, because I knew, givingwise, I was still way out in front.

But then I thought again. I reached out and put my hand on his shoulder, feeling the warmth of his skin radiating beneath his clean white shirt.

"Sure," I said. "Thanks."

CHAPTER 13
THE HOLLOWNESS OF HALLOWEEN

Nine-year-olds love Halloween. For weeks before the big day they plan their costumes, mentally rehearsing different disguises 'til they find the one that fits both their sense of the outrageous and their sense of themselves.

Goblins, vampires, ghosts, and zombies. If you're from the comic-book phase of character development, Skeletor, Flash, Superman (or woman), and the Hulk. Or, if you're from the postmodernist school of Halloween as social commentary, then Madonna, Twisted Sister, Earth Firster, Acter-Upper.

But for nine-year-old Isaac, Halloween, like so many other things, is about friends.

Weeks earlier my Isaac presented me with an elaborate plan whereby he and two buddies, in a coordinated effort, would successfully cover the entire local neighborhood, allowing maximum candy intake. The two friends were athletic boys slightly older than he, compatriots to whom he pointed with pride.

"Frank will go up here, and George will go this way," Isaac said with a serious demeanor, rotating the paper on the kitchen table. "Then we'll switch off. Finally, we'll meet here at the corner and divide all the candy up equally." He liked the companionship, and he liked the sharing, and he particularly liked the fact that it came out even.

Every day was a subtraction problem waiting to happen. "Dad, how many days till Halloween?" Isaac asked on, say, the seventeenth of October. "You figure it out," I responded.

"Frank and George and me are going out together," he said. "No offense, Dad, but I don't think I want to go out with you this Halloween."

"That's okay," I answered, watching another milestone pass into the void. "I'll just check in on you every once in a while, if you don't mind."

At last the blessed day arrived. As soon as his eyelids cracked open Isaac bounced out of bed and was ready to go. Unfortunately, twelve long hours lay between the present and trick-or-treating time. He was told to clean his room once, twice, seventeen times at escalating volumes before sufficient concentration allowed success.

In the early afternoon he at last lifted the receiver of the phone in the kitchen to contact his friends and finalize the evening's strategy. He called the older of his two buddies first.

Though he stretched the cord as far as it would go in a search for privacy I overheard some of the conversation.

"What do you mean you're going out with George?" Isaac's voice said, surprised. "George and I made a plan for us all to go out together."

There was silence on his end. My son paced a bit closer, turned rapidly, then strode again out to the end of the cord. He flopped down in a chair, stood up again.

"But Frank, why can't we all . . . we planned . . . oh . . . but why not?. . .but, Frank, hey, we could, . . . oh . . . oh . . . okay."

He hung up the phone. He grinned a tight grin at me. With a tense gleam in his eye, he said, "Now I'm gonna call George." Isaac is not one to surrender his dreams easily.

We still have one of those old rotary dials. He dialed the numbers hurriedly, made a mistake, hung up, dialed again. He got George on the phone, paced hastily out to the end of the cord.

"George, you remember our plan?" From where I stood wiping off the kitchen counter I heard the excitement, and anxiety, in his voice.

"Now Frank is saying . . . yeah, but why don't we all. But George, don't you remember how we talked about our plan." He walked back toward the kitchen. He was speaking more audibly now, in a loud hissing whisper. "But we talked about it first! George, how about if we . . . "

I walked over to where he was standing by the phone and bent over 'til my mouth was close beside his free ear. "Let it go, guy," I whispered. "We'll go out with your brother and have a good time."

He walked away from me out to the end of the cord.

"Okay," he said into the phone, "Okay. Okay!"

He hung up the phone, hard.

He turned away and walked up the center staircase. His face looked all right. I finished cleaning up the kitchen.

A minute or two later I went upstairs to see how Aaron was doing in cleaning his room. Isaac, whose bed was on the other side of the long attic space, was nowhere to be seen.

On the way down the stairs I noticed the door to the computer room was closed. I walked in and there was Isaac, seated silently before the glowing screen. He was using a drawing program, moving the mouse to create dark words on a background of light. I saw by his creased brow that he was concentrating hard on what he was doing.

Here is what he drew:

> I wish I
> Never had
> Friends

It was at the moment that he drew a big, dark X over the word "Friends" that he finally became a little boy again and broke down. I pulled him off the seat into my arms and he cried and cried and cried. He grieved his wonderful lost plans and his dreams like we all grieve our lost plans and dreams, except his soft, vulnerable little nine-year-old heart grieved a lot more sincerely and openly.

Aaron, who fights with his older brother incessantly, came into the room and stood silently, close behind his sobbing older brother.

I worked hard not to tell him that it didn't matter, that we would have a better time without his stupid old friends, because I knew that to him it did matter, it mattered very much, and it was in the terrible, inevitable order of things that he had to be sad about it.

He was sad because his two best friends were acting as if they liked each other more than they liked him, and that hurt. It always hurts when we learn we're not loved by everyone as much as in our secret hearts we want to be loved. It hurts when the world presents its hard edge to our soft parts. Just because it hurts doesn't mean it's not real, and just because it's real doesn't mean it doesn't hurt. Sometimes, particularly if you're nine years old, there's just no getting away from it.

After a while, as is also in the order of things, he stopped crying and pulled himself together and we talked about the fun the three of us were going to have trick-or-treating that night. And we did have fun, racing around like maniacs to every house with a light on.

As for Isaac, he forgave George and Frank even before he put much of a dent in that small mountain of candy. He forgave much more easily and freely than his father—and his forgiveness meant there was no hurt in his soft young heart that would make any part of it old and hard.

Susanna Hepburn Knavitz

CHAPTER 14
THE CAT'S LESSON

From the way Isaac slouched into the room, head hung low, I could tell it was bad news.

He stood before me, shuffling his feet for a moment. Then he came out with it. Something about the cat.

"What?" I said, an edge creeping into my voice.

He mumbled again. "Speak up!" I shouted.

He shouted, "I just pee-ed on the cat!"

"You pee-ed on the cat?" I repeated. "Pee-ed on the cat?"

"Yes, yes!" he shouted again. "I pee-ed on the cat!"

I just didn't get it. You can pee in the toilet, you can pee in your pants, you can pee off a deck into the cool night breeze, but pee on a cat? It put me right into a trance.

Then it started to make sense. Ever since our cat was a tiny kitten, whenever he hears the tinkle of pee into the waiting waters of the toilet he rushes through the bathroom door—left ajar by hurried children—puts his paws up on the rim of the toilet, and peers down into the bowl. I guess he is fascinated by the play of lights and waves as the pee hits the water.

But what at first was an innocent foible had in time become an odious problem. As the cat grew larger he began not only peeking meekly at the descending torrent, he would extend much of his feline body over the edge of the toilet and down into the bowl itself. He did not want to miss a single shining drop.

Then the effort was to miss him. Since the cat usually raced into the bathroom and hurled himself against the toilet while the pee-er was in midstream, the relieving human was faced with an immediate choice: either attempt the feat of peeing into the tiny aperture left uncovered by cat or arrest the flow and carry out a dance as one shifted continually from one foot to the other and shooed the cat away from the bowl to protect it from further intrusions. Meanwhile, one struggled for a better angle of entry.

As the reader can imagine, both alternatives had their down side in terms of bathroom mess. And the process of decision itself was a terrible obligation, coming as it did at a ritual moment of peace and relaxation, sacred for as long as man has worried about stains on his pants.

But there is a solution, clear and simple to all mature minds.

Close the bathroom door after entering.

Of course, like most simple answers, it was widely ignored. Simple answers in general fail to engage people's intelligence and their sense of curiosity, their cleverness, their deviousness, their need for challenge. There is a sense that simple answers are made to be ignored, and thereby man introduces excitement and complexity to life.

But there is a point at which people are supposed to learn to accept simple answers. It's the end of childhood, when boys and girls can legitimately be called young men and women. It's a time when their bodies grow bigger and heavier and they stand before you like a slightly miniature version of real humanoids, and one begins to expect that they may be capable of something.

At the end of childhood what was once cute is now infuriating. Making a mess while eating, throwing clothes on the floor, making strange, spontaneous sounds at all hours of the day and night, all those behaviors that once elicited a statement like, "Oh, isn't he adorable!" now engender hard glares and the occasional full-throated lecture.

Of course, these changes occur exclusively in the minds of adults. The child simply finds himself dropped on the planet and is rolling along, taking it day by day, when suddenly he is confronted with this strange new concept called—RESPONSIBILITY.

We parents falsely assume that just because a child reaches the age of reason a light goes on in a child's head and at moments of decision he will knit his brow and think, "Well now, is it right to hit my brother? Is it the best thing for myself, my family, my future?"

No, he is simply a "big child," looming where once he darted, beginning to develop the mental potential to control a body as big as that of a small adult. Unfortunately, for him, physics says that with size comes mass, with mass comes power, and with power comes responsibility.

Responsibility to bring your plate to the sink, to make your bed, to perform various low-status chores that related adults would like, if possible, to avoid.

Responsibility to say what you mean and mean what you say. To stand up against temptation. To follow the road of righteousness wherever it may lead.

And, at all times and in all circumstances, to avoid pee-ing on the cat.

For, as we all know, pee-ing on a cat is bad.

But washing a cat is much, much worse.

Susanna Hepburn Knautz

CHAPTER 15
NO FREE BUTTONS

It was as he was getting dressed one recent morning that Aaron spilled the terrible secret. He began by way of a question.

"Dad," he said innocently. "Do you like pushing buttons?"

I gave some typical parental response, like, "Uh-huh" or "Sure" or "Come on, hurry up!"

"I love pushing buttons," he went on dreamily. "It's so neat. You just push a button and something happens."

I began to suspect we were going somewhere. I let the silence hang for a few seconds.

"Dad," he said finally, his voice heavy with guilt. "I pushed the button on the camera."

There it was. He pushed the button on the camera. He knew he wasn't supposed to push the button on the camera. But nonetheless he went right ahead and pushed the button on the camera.

As a matter of fact, it was a brand-new camera whose button had never before been pushed, the first real grown-up camera his grown-up parents had ever owned, purchased just that week by my wife and me for the specific purpose of photographing slides to accompany a future teaching presentation.

I was confronted with the confusion faced by every parent forced to deal with a confession. Do you mete out punishment for the deed confessed or do you issue a reward for the noble act of confessing it?

It was not the first time we had faced this quandary. On another recent night we returned home to discover that someone had pushed the button on some hair stuff, spraying white foam into the recesses of the bathroom.

"Okay," I shouted. "Who sprayed the white stuff?"

There was silence. I could hear the gears turning as Isaac and Aaron silently negotiated who was going to take the fall. But, probably because we had discovered the offense rather than allowing a confession to emerge in its own good time, no acknowledgment was forthcoming. The silent negotiations didn't work any better than the verbal ones.

We sent the children to bed, swearing they would remain there for the rest of their natural lives if necessary, until somebody stood tall—or at least as tall as he could—and shouldered the burden of guilt.

Still no confession. The children got on their beds and sat there, looking as if they were prepared to wait this one out.

We tried the good-cop bad-cop routine. My gentle wife promised that there would be no punishment—no consequences whatsoever—for the guilty party. We just wanted to *talk to them.*

"I did it! I did it!" both said simultaneously, leaping from their beds.

I scrutinized them, each in his turn. This is an old trick my mother used on me, this sense that a parent can look into your eyes and pierce your very soul to determine if you are telling the truth. In the case of my own children, however, it seems only to be teaching them to be better liars. Which, of course, is a skill eminently suited for the modern world.

"No," they acknowledged, one after another, "I just said I did it so I could get out of bed."

Then we were faced with a larger, deeper philosophical problem. Which was the truth: the admission of the offense or their denial of that admission? Or both? Or neither? We were rapidly sliding down a slippery surface of hair stuff into a convoluted, Alice-in-Wonderland world of reversed realities and transparent truths.

Outthought, we retreated into our own minds and beds. Sleep, and its accompanying forgetfulness, was the best cure. We were learning that confessions, except in the back rooms of South American police stations, come in their own time. Force things, and you end up with bruises and mere words.

Just a few days ago Aaron's love for buttons gave him another profound human experience. While at a local mall my wife urged the children to wander among the stores while she finished up some business.

The children, of course, made their way directly to the video arcade. Once inside, Aaron, caught up in the excitement of flashing lights, flying money, and frenzied action, began plunking his coins into the machines. The games were good, the lights beautiful, the buttons wonderful to push.

In no time—about six minutes, at fifty cents a whack—his $4.50, resolutely saved over many a week's allowance, was gone. It was irretrievably gone, swallowed up deep inside machines to purchase a few moments' fun, and now there was nothing left. The subsequent plan, to go to the toy store and purchase some deeply desired, garishly painted piece of plastic, was in ashes.

A few moments later he confronted his mother, his face a mixture of anger and grief. It was hard, hard for her not to salve his pain by replacing the money, hard for her to let him have his little lesson of pain and loss. But she did it, and maybe he learned on his own that this button-pushing pleasure has its price.

So, back with Aaron, I decided to take the soft road. "Well, what did you take a picture of?"

About this he was quite serious. "I didn't take a picture of the floor or the chair or anything," he said, "I was careful. I took a picture out the window."

The image of Aaron standing by the window, pulse racing with the suspense of secret action as he studiously arranged his single shot, all so he could experience the bliss of pushing another button, led me down the path to forgiveness.

"Well, I hope it was a good picture."

So, if during our next presentation you find yourself viewing a slide of our front window, the driveway beyond, a snowbank, and a few bare, tilted trees, you will understand.

CHAPTER 16
THE BIRTH OF ISAAC

It was midnight plus one second on Isaac's due date that my wife's water broke and spread across the mattress in a warm, wet pool. The invasion of dampness awakened me. Miriam made a high, surprised sound—"Oh!"—that somehow combined aspects both of pleasure and anxiety. Suddenly and after long expectation we knew we were off on a journey we desperately hoped would be full of wonder and joy; but my Irish negativism told me one thing for certain—if it wasn't good, it was going to be very, very bad.

Months earlier we had decided to have the baby at our ramshackle, clapboard home in rural Texas. My wife, a risk taker, believed passionately in the healthful properties of home birth. Me, I fretted and nagged, visualizing a catastrophe. I wasn't yet aware of facts like that the Netherlands, which has an infant mortality rate far lower than our own, gives birth to 70% of her children at home. I only knew that what we were doing was, by American standards, weird—and if one of my kids died because I did something weird, my Gaelic guilt would burn forever.

The deciding factor, I acknowledge with shame, was money. Like forty million other Americans, we had no health insurance, and for us paupers it was much cheaper to have the baby at home. One thousand dollars covered the whole deal—prenatal exams, birthing classes, and the birth itself. For a broke Irishman it was like hearing that an uncle had just died and left you a horse.

It was midnight plus five minutes when I feverishly dialed the midwives' telephone number. Now, Texas is a lot of different things to a lot of different people, but the one thing it is for everyone is big. They told me it would take about two and a half hours for them to get to our house.

Miriam's strong, clear contractions were about four minutes apart. You didn't have to be a Rhodes scholar—and I wasn't—to realize that if the birthing process proceeded apace I would end up playing the part of Dr. Zhivago. Gently replacing the phone in its cradle—excuse the foreshadowing—my first impulse was to fall apart and begin the process of blaming, which would extend years into the future.

"Why did you have to talk me into this crazy idea?" I would shout. "How come I always have to be the *rational* one? Just because I almost have a doctoral degree do you think I know thing one about how to get a baby from inside you to the outside world? No! No! I can't even believe that it happens at all! It's a deep, mysterious process that should be handled by deep, mysterious people! Would you have me bite off the umbilical cord with my teeth and circumcise him with *my safety razor?*"

I looked to where Miriam lay on our bed, happy, excited, and, yes, expectant. Sensitivities honed over years of training told me this was not the time to fall apart.

So we made brownies. We sauntered around the kitchen, in the quiet small hours of the morning, moving with the practiced care of meditating monks, speaking in whispers, soundlessly arranging the bowls and pans and spoons. It was ritual time. The contractions slowed. We relaxed.

At 2:45 A.M. the midwives arrived in force, with their assistants and the children of their assistants, with party hats and kazoos and confetti and one red hat with tiny electric lights all around it, mine to wear as long as I dared. The contractions took off again slowly, like a pelican struggling to raise its big body from the surface of a lake.

Soon the work of the birthing process was in full swing. Miriam lay on the bed, propped up on pillows, breathing through contractions of increasing intensity. I knelt over her, gazing into her eyes, matching my breathing to her own. Again and again we focused on images of "opening" and "down." I moved my hands in a flowing, backhanded motion over her shoulders and belly and hips, all the while whispering, "down," "open," "relaxed and smooth," and the like in time to her slow, deep breathing. Her need allowed me to have some effect.

Meanwhile, she labored with increasing passion; occasionally, she grasped my hand and squeezed, hard, digging her nails into my palm. During one difficult period I massaged her lower back and hips, then withdrew as the next moment she could not stand to be touched, then came forward again as we reestablished the rhythm of our breathing.

"Down; open and down; smooth and relaxed and open." When Miriam experienced an intense need to urinate I helped her to the toilet, where she sat in blissful relief as I sat on the edge of the tub, holding her hands and gazing into her eyes. We have not since shared a bathroom experience as intimately.

The midwives called out measurements, arranged Miriam's body this way and that. At one point with labor well advanced and the top of the baby's head just visible, things got stuck; progress slowed and Miriam appeared, for the first time, to be experiencing real discomfort.

Was there some dreaded problem, I wondered? Is this when the nightmare starts? The pain, the complications, the ambulances, the surgery, the regret and the guilt and the grief? Is this where the wonder of the beginning of life ends and the anxious, fretful encounter with finitude begins? We shared the panic of this transition.

The midwives now were laboring also, serious and intent. We helped Miriam off the bed and supported her as she hunkered down on the floor like a southern farmer drawing directions in the dirt. She went through a couple of contractions in this position then struggled back onto the bed.

The crisis was past, the corner rounded, and the flow of life continued apace.

At 6:36 A.M., with the light of dawn shining through the worn curtains and morning birds warming up their song, Isaac Joseph came into the world.

As he emerged, slowly at first and then with a great rush, I learned what it meant to have "a catch in your throat"; it was a tiny inhalation that happens when you're overcome with, yes, FEELINGS. Of course, I was frightened, not by any of the circumstances of the birth but rather by the unexpected power of emotion. Then I surrendered and again beheld Isaac, at nine pounds four a perfectly formed linebacker of the future. The midwives put him up to Miriam's breast, where he nursed for a moment, she smiling and weeping like the winner of a great marathon; then the midwives severed the cord and gave him to me.

At the midwives' instruction, I took Isaac into the kitchen, where we guys were alone for a while. I first noticed his eyes: calm and clear, none of the "What am I doing in this crazy place?" sort of birth trauma. Just a pure, balanced vision of the world as his happy eyes traveled from the lamp on the kitchen ceiling, to the bright light of the window, to me.

This next part is really true; I mean, the rest is true as well, but you might have a hard time believing this part so I'm reassuring you that it is fact.

As Isaac lay on my lap drinking in the world with his eyes a simple, happy word came out of his mouth.

He said, "Hi!"

He must have known I was stunned, so he repeated it a few times, in each instance addressing a newly noticed part of the world.

"Hi! Hi!" he said. Then he looked right at me through his clear, new gray eyes. "Hi!"

Pierced to the bone, I bent close to warm skin and smelled his perfect infant's breath, the first of a hundred thousand times I would do this during his young life, and felt my heart leap toward that of my new son.

"Hi. Hi, Isaac," I croaked, as best I could through my tears. "Welcome to the world."

Susanna Hepburn-Knaith

CHAPTER 17
THE DUAL POWER OF IMAGINATION

Five-year-old Aaron appeared like a ghost beside my bed in an early morning haze of sleep and dawn. He stood there, a silent wraith outlined in the white light of the window behind him. Finally I felt his presence and lifted an eyelid.

He spotted the light glistening off my exposed eye. "Daddy," he whispered, "I'm scared!"

I groggily pulled myself up on an elbow. "What're you afraid of, Aaron?"

Aaron shifted from bare foot to foot on the cold floor, then continued in hushed tones, "Everything is different and it's moving around and it's scary."

"It's just your imagination," I muttered, flopping back onto the pillow, "gettin' out of control."

On recent mornings Aaron again and again has appeared beside my bed and I have followed him back to his room in the gathering light and shaken out the bathrobes, which, drooping on their hooks, look like goblins, run a broom under the bed where gargoyles dwell, pulled back the concealing curtain to reveal—nothing.

And this time, once again, Aaron is not to be dissuaded. "Daddy," he says, "how come we can't control our imagination?"

Now, Aaron knows that the best way to drag me into wakefulness is to hook my mind up to some intriguing philosophical inquiry. Indeed, I wonder, why can't we control our imagination? Why, when you tell a child bothered by terrors to go off to bed and think about Christmas, good friends, baseball, and other pleasantries, does he invariably shriek in reply, "But I can't!"

No, there is a part of our imagination that extends beyond us, that seems to have a life of its own, and that will drag us reluctantly to places we would rather not visit. Children are frequent guests in this mysterious place.

Aaron is continuing his whispered confession.

"Sometimes in the dark the bureau looks like a dragon and then sometimes I go up to it and feel it all over and then I see it's not a dragon—it's just a bureau!" He says this with the hushed awe appropriate to a magical act, then hesitates and goes on in words so soft they scarcely reach my ear. "But then sometimes I'm too scared to touch it."

Yes, yes, sometimes imagination brings us visions so unsettling that we dare not carry out the investigative work required to discover if they are truth or illusion. And so they hang there, these scary things, present but unevaluated, perhaps even unacknowledged, growing ever more threatening in their darkness.

Then, after falling off to sleep we have a nightmare and we wake up screaming or in a cold sweat. In that moment, jerking erect in bed, we know we must face the fear, we must dare to touch it, we must dare to discover, is it a bureau—or is it indeed a dragon?

So we reach a trembling hand into the darkness, we reach out, and . . .

For children, deprived as yet of the small habits and rituals that give our grown-up days their certain shape, bereft of the history of having pulled back the curtain ten thousand times and found nothing, this darkness is even more threatening—but Aaron's whispered words describing the terrifying bureau say it more clearly.

"Sometimes the handles look like they're moving. But when it's light out I can see the handles so it's not so scary."

His imagination—any living imagination—is the site of a struggle between light and darkness, between fear and knowledge, and our fevered intention carts its candle of illumination into the scary places.

And so with a grunt I again accompany Aaron off to his room to fondle the shadowed edges of the bureau and flatten storm-enshrouded blanket mountain peaks, until he is certain that no monster lurks therein.

Later that same day Aaron sits in the front yard, pretending that a pile of logs is a spaceship. He shouts up to where I stand on a ladder painting a window.

"You know, Daddy, having a good imagination can be great, too!"

Yes, imagination can be great; it can be your best friend and boon companion—except during those long, lonely nights, when your own mind unveils what you would rather not see.

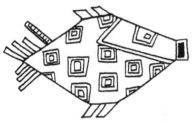

CHAPTER 18
THE MYTH AND REALITY
OF QUALITY TIME

Having come from a large family in an era of large families I was always a little irritated by vaguely self-righteous discussions about "quality time." In the teeming neighborhoods in which most of us baby boomers grew up you were pretty much on your own by age seven. Adult attention, quality or no, was hard to come by and was usually accompanied by the pain of punishment. Adults appeared to live in a strange and separate world, and we kids, whether hanging out in a "fort"—a few boards thrown over a fence behind a garage—or scoping out the recesses of some well-traveled urban park, strove to solidify that separation at every opportunity.

I think we felt the forced independence helped to make us more resourceful, tougher. We had to survive on the streets because the only alternative was the alien far-distant world of adults, adults who would eye each other and us strangely if we sought to share our small problems. Of course, then the adults knew that the streets were essentially a haven—unlike today, when many neighborhoods are as dangerous as a battlefront and their children as traumatized as shell-shocked veterans.

So I thought of "quality time" as a bourgeois indulgence, an invention of wealthy yuppies who need relief from the guilt they feel at spending their time on ambition rather than their children.

Now, as I stroke my gray-flecked beard and watch six-year-old son

Isaac draw his name in the snow with a stick, I feel differently. After etching his own name, he draws those of his two brothers, his mother, and me. Then he stands back: "That's our whole family!" he exclaims, emphasizing for himself a basic truth; the five of us are separate from everyone else—we are a family.

Then he goes to the swing, supplying me with a running narrative of his thoughts: "I feel like I'm gonna fly right over the bar!" He jumps off the swing and rolls in the snow, heedless, country boy that he is, of the mud and wet. I know that he knows I am watching, and this is a very private performance by an actor whom, the more I watch him, the more comfortable he becomes in his role. And his role is precisely to be himself, that very special person whom Mr. Rogers rightly says has never been before and will never be again. I am honored by the performance.

As I watch him I know that this, indeed, is quality time, time that communicates to my son that he is a person worth watching, time that serves to "confirm his identity." I realize that quality time is time that allows a child to be a child, to play at the performance of himself, so that someday he too can be that strange form of intelligent known as "a grown-up" and watch and confirm his own children as they demonstrate their absolute uniqueness. This special empathic human capacity—the ability to see and to some extent feel the world as another sees and feels it—is a quality that appears to be sadly lacking in this era of quality time.

I know too that quality time is short and all too infrequent. Quality time needs to be long enough so that the child will not feel that he needs to "perform" in a negative sense, as before a stranger with whom he is uncomfortable. Quality time needs to happen often enough that the child knows this is not his last performance, that he will be seen again and again and again. How to obtain such long and frequent periods is a problem that falls heavily in the lap of concerned adults.

A lot of productive child-watching used to be done by grandparents, before grandparents disappeared about the same time as

those safe neighborhoods. There used to be someone who had
the time to sit and watch, to calmly sit and watch and notice the subtle
developments in the drama of the family, someone who could take it
all in day after day. Now that Grandma lives a couple of time zones
away the watching chair is empty and beckoning; if filled at all, it is
too often occupied by harried adults who want only to get the
watching job done so they can finally take a moment to look at
themselves.

For quality time to be truly quality it must be freely given, free of
expectations or recriminations. And if survival pressures mean it
cannot be measured in hours then perhaps sometime between the
getting up and putting to bed a moment must be taken, a moment or
three to watch and appreciate, a moment to supply a wink and some
warm applause.

CHAPTER 19
BUGS, BOYS AND BIRTHINGS

There it is! Can't you *see* it? Right there on the windowsill! It's got six legs and four wings!"

I lifted my eyes from the plate I had just withdrawn from the warm water of the sink and looked at the window sash. I tried to spot what Isaac was pointing out,but all I could see was the dirty ledge and the smudged glass of the window.

"It's right there! On the wood!" Isaac, standing by my elbow at the sink, persisted.

Then, as I continued staring at the spot where Isaac was frenziedly pointing it appeared as if from nowhere, emerging suddenly from the brown background of the sash—a long, skinny, orange insect with six legs and four translucent wings.

Isaac ran off to get the insect identification book and returned, riffling pages. I continued washing dishes. Five-year-old Aaron appeared silently at my left elbow.

"Here it is!" Isaac called out, stopping at a page. "It's a falcon mosquito!" he cried. "Let's whap it, 'cuz those things can bite you real bad! An' besides, there's millions of 'em."

"No, no!" Aaron piped up from my other side. "Carry it outside! It's a living bug! It's bad to kill a living bug!"

The debate was on. Was it permissible to wallop something that at some future date might bite you? Or is it invariably wrong to kill a living bug? Did the fact that there are uncounted millions of bugs make their lives less precious, less valuable?

It seemed right for these small boys to be having such an argument, considering that nine out of ten acts of violence in the United States are committed by young men, and we're growing a few of them in our house.

The problems with males start even before birth, with "male vulnerability": More males than females die before and during birth, and more males than females experience complications in the birth process, resulting in a significantly higher rate of male birth defects. Interestingly, the mother's birth labor with a male baby lasts an average of an hour longer—and long labor is positively correlated with behavioral problems in later life.

A controversial explanation of male vulnerability states that women during pregnancy develop antibodies against the male fetus, resulting in damage; that is, men have more problems because they are born of women. Unfortunately, there aren't many options in this regard.

A more hopeful line of explanation regarding male differences examines variations in child-rearing practices, under the old observation that you become what you do. During childhood, girls receive praise for being nurturant and caring whereas boys get reinforcement for being "tough." Caring for infants and small children develops nurturant impulses in the caregiver.

It is for this reason that the financial need for a two-income family and the consequent requirement that men assume a more prominent role in child care is a hopeful transition for society. The man who provides loving daily care for a child is not the man who rapes, robs, and pillages. We can help our boys overcome their "male vulnerability" by rewarding them for being caring as well as for being tough, and in the long run we will be doing our part to rectify the violence of our culture.

And what was the fate of the four-winged, six-legged, translucent winged living bug that brought up this discussion? I have to admit that after a period of tortured debate Isaac struck it no harder than he has been known to hit his little brother—just to much worse effect.

CHAPTER 20
WHAT JUSTIFIES THE PAIN

B e warned. This one is going to be mushy. It will talk about love and human relationships in the sentimental manner hard-hearted types find so offensive. Among the vulnerable and yielding, a tear may drop and darken the pale pages.

This story is about the power of the bond between parents and children. It's a power that people who do not have children can never comprehend as they stand smirking off to the side while your two-year-old presses toast into the VCR; they sigh with relief as your sixteen-year-old screams an obscenity and slams the door on his way into the night.

It's about the power that would lead a father to take a bullet for his child and die happy. It's about the power that leads a parent to go off each day to long hours at a job he doesn't like much—but feels certain is worth each miserable hour when his child comes shining through the door.

I, personally, think it has something to do with children's faces. You let your eyes rest on your child's face while they're watching television or performing some other mindless activity and you feel a closeness to them that exceeds any other relationship. In their face you can see reflected every noble, loving, dignified inclination you've ever had minus all the foolish nonsense you've been blind or weak or angry enough to allow yourself to believe. You look at your child's face and a voice in you says, "Yeah, yeah, now I remember—that's what it's all about."

So right then, while they're staring at *Sesame Street* or *The Simpsons*, you reach over and pass a weathered hand over his smooth forehead and across his cheek or maybe you ruffle his hair and he goes, "Daa-aad! Cut it out!" Or maybe—this was my father's favorite male-ploy-for-showing-affection-without-having-to-say-anything-mushy—you reach over while driving and whap him on the left knee with your right hand and then squeeze a little bit while he laughs and squeals and squirms.

Or maybe when he falls asleep on your lap you bend over and whisper those three words into his incredibly detailed, perfect little ear—"I love you."

Okay, okay, I know. I'm going pretty far. I'll pull back on the mushy stuff but you have to understand one thing: This hurts me as much as it hurts you.

But the part that really hurts about having children is the fear. There's fear of nuclear and biological holocaust. There's fear of drunk drivers. There's fear of drugs and disease and meteors and lightning and falling trees. There's terrible, dreadful fear of anything that could by some awful chance discombobulate the narrow risk that keeps your child alive and leave you one of those sad, sad people condemned to live the rest of your life with a hole in your heart.

That's the terrible thing about having kids and realizing that you love them absolutely and overwhelmingly. It's the realization that by loving them you pass a part of your vulnerability on to someone else over whom, in the final analysis, you have no control. You realize that by loving you can be had. Your love can be held hostage by heartless circumstance or bad guys with warped-out eyes. By loving you extend the frontiers of yourself, and since Caesar discovered Gaul was divided into four parts everyone has known that defending frontiers is dangerous business.

It's much easier, then, not to do it, to avoid having children or, if you do, to avoid loving them in a way that puts you on the front line. It's easier to be cool, to be distant, to stay far away and watch the parade pass, now with a snicker, now with a guffaw. It's easier to stay tucked within yourself because, Lord knows, just keeping yourself in one piece these days is difficult enough.

I like to say that having kids is the only joy capable of justifying the pain and risk of having kids.

Modern life tends to say that you shouldn't care, that you shouldn't spread out your heart to include others. All the twelve-step stuff about taking responsibility for yourself has gotten twisted into caring only about yourself—a fundamental misconstrual of the difference between power and human feeling. It may be true that you cannot take care of anyone else if you are unable to take care of yourself . . . but it applies to everyone except your children.

Anyway, it doesn't matter. What I really mean is that the difference doesn't matter but the love does matter, probably more than anything else, because when your child comes running through the door, face ablaze with excitement, holding a tiny tooth in his hand and shouting, "Daddy! Daddy!" well, all the self-protective thoughts and plans don't matter any more than a pair of galoshes in a tidal wave—it's love at first sight, again.

CHAPTER 21
FROM SMILEY FACE TO STAR

Isaac is a creature of the sun. When he draws pictures of people they are, usually, stick figures. Isaac's people stand with arms raised and outstretched, fingers extended, the neckline topped by a hugely beaming face. But when the clouds come to his young soul the sun is obscured and darkness rules his wide countenance; the shining face is plunged instantaneously into darkest night.

I have often been so moved by the depth and terrible honesty of Isaac's grief that I am ready to give him whatever he desires—a third candy bar, his brother's toy—if only to stem the prodigious and heartrending flow of tears.

When I was a child if I performed some academic task particularly well the teacher might place on my forehead a silver star; I remember walking slowly back to my seat, eyes slightly crossed as I attempted to focus on this sign of honor.

These days teachers utilize a smiley face—or frowney face—to render judgment. Today, as Isaac returns from school, his mouth is a horizontal line; he hands me a tiny piece of purple paper and on it are stamped both the smiley and frowney faces, along with the words, "Isaac had a terrible morning" then "Isaac had a great afternoon!"

Like fathers down through the ages I slowly wheel around from my work and assume the judge's mantle. Isaac searches my face for a hint of choice. Clearly, he knows, judgment had been rendered; in the morning he was less than perfect. Father/Judge must now decide:

What is the sentence?

Moving backward through the legal process, Isaac then presents what he hopes is exculpatory data. It is the usual story, as familiar to football players as first graders: The other guy struck first, he retaliated, and the authorities caught him. It's not fair, but it's true. He is as innocent as he appears.

Sure, kid. The Murphy Court now resembles New York Municipal: judgment is swift, sentencing largely arbitrary. Isaac is found guilty of Getting Himself Somehow Involved in a Problematic Situation Without Forethought, a household misdemeanor. The sentence: No Nintendo for twenty-four hours.

In a moment the sunny sky turns black, tropical rains pour. Isaac loves his Nintendo, treasures its many and maddening diversions. Like a judge who knows the local park needs cleaning and therefore assigns any and all to community service, I suspend Nintendo for the most unrelated offenses. But Isaac's grief of loss is real. That which he loves has been taken away. "I am innocent, don't you understand?" he pleads. "Don't you believe me? You never believe me!"

The Appeals Court is slowly drawing into session; perhaps the lower court judge was a bit overhasty, even callous and excessive—that judge has been known at times to be downright nasty, boorish, and mean. Why, he's had seventy-two of his decisions overturned this year alone!

But, no! This one will stand. Even in the crestfallen face of grief and loss, this one must stand, if only out of respect for the principle of law. "That's not fair!" shouts Isaac, his tears drying in the heat of rage. "You never believe me! I hate you! I'm going to run away from home!"

Contempt! Thou shalt not show contempt for the law! Watch yourself or I'll have you thrown into your bed for two hours! No Nintendo for a week! The law has ways of commanding respect!

Distraught with grief and anger, Isaac stomps up the stairs, his small knees churning. "I'll disappear up the chimney like a backwards Santa!" he shouts in parting, regaining a measure of self-respect if not liberty.

Downstairs alone, my docket clear again, I take a moment to examine my conscience. In truth, I hate this goddamn job, this judge's job of distancing and punishing my sweet child. Smiley face indeed! Frowney face, pshaw! It seems that today's teachers are more desirous by far of quiet classrooms than passionate learning.

It is well known that boys are significantly more active (and aggressive) than girls. It is likewise known that better than nine out of ten elementary school teachers are women; women who were, at one time, little girls—not little boys. It is entirely possible that before a male child has learned how to read he has already become adept at hiding his proud boy spirit deep inside himself.

The star of my youth somehow connoted divine beneficence, a bounty no more anthropomorphic than a stone. The smiley face of today is in reality the teacher's face, the externalization of her momentary emotional state: she smiles upon "appropriate behavior" or she frowns upon rambunctiousness, conflict, dirt, anger, rebelliousness, intemperance, loudness, greed, and every other boyish impulse. The stamp of frowney face is pressed upon them all, and thus all obstreperous impulses migrate outward first into the schoolyard and thence, forever frowning, into the streets, psychiatric offices, jails, and recovery centers of the community beyond.

As fathers invest their soul in parenting and soon after send their child to school they see arrayed before them the legion of female teachers with whom their sons must march—most of them well-meaning but all of them carrying the burden of their fathers with them, as every man does his mother. Every teacher brings her feelings about men, their dirt, their bullishness, their sex. The father who goes to confer with his son's teacher usually returns not with a star but with raised blood pressure, one small step closer to the bursting that will signal his end.

Meanwhile, Isaac's sobbing has finally ceased; he has served some of his sentence and my heart tells me that he is deserving of time off for general lovableness. Maybe we'll go for a walk or play some catch or bring in some wood. In truth, I have need right now to see his smiling face again, gleaming like an evening star, bright, long and low on the horizon.

Susanna Hepburn Knavez

CHAPTER 22
THE SPIRITUAL SHOWER

Aaron is a painfully early riser. Five seconds after the slightest sound disturbs his slumber, before even the mist has risen from the valley below our home, his small feet hit the floor and he's up, investigating. As we read stories about Curious George, the meddlesome monkey, Aaron made the comment, "When I wake up, I get curious!" My own conflicting desires to sleep and to support his burgeoning curiosity prevent me from simply—and fruitlessly—shouting, "Back to bed!"

What this means is that Aaron and I shower together in the morning. While I shampoo my hair, Aaron stands in the warm flow drawing pictures in the beads of moisture on the porcelain tiles. Four-year-olds are good to shower with because they're still short enough to stand in the drain end of a standard tub and not block copious amounts of water; plus the water can be steaming hot—the way I like it—and by the time it reaches down to Aaron's level it's cool enough for him. Physics, at this moment, is exceedingly fair.

Usually Aaron is silent in the shower, or maybe he hums a low tune. He's off in a reverieland reserved exclusively for entranced four-year-olds.

But this morning, soon after the water is roaring and the swirls of steam rise above the curtainrod, Aaron blurts out something that has been on his curious mind.

"Daddy," he says. "You know, Isaac thinks spirits are real."

My partially gray head perceives this as a leading statement
beneath which lurks untold mysteries, and like most gray heads mine
has learned that if it keeps silent time will pass and the mystery can be
avoided.

But Aaron isn't going to let me drift away like a listener
disinterested in the diatribe of some state fair hawker. I remember,
many years ago, a slick young man stood before a huge crowd at a
fair; drawn by the numbers I joined the group and listened to his
numbing spiel for a few minutes, wondering how he had accumulated
such a following.

Then I noticed that each time someone attempted to detach himself
from the group the salesman from his high podium called out,
engaging the individual in conversation, focusing upon him the
attention of some hundred-odd observers. In the carnival-colored night
the escapees looked back, caught in the glare of the crowd, bumbling
their replies to the hawker's smooth inquiries. After a few such
painful spectacles few dared risk an escape, and so we stood there,
sheepishly, 'til he was done. Maybe, I thought, this is not only how
we come to buy but also how we come to believe.

In like fashion Aaron caught me up as I attempted my passive
getaway.

"So, Dad," he says. "Is it true? Are spirits real?"

Warm water beat the back of my neck as my thoughts accelerated
from zero to sixty. Aaron waited below, washed by the waterfall from
my body.

My immediate but unspoken response was, "Well, how do I know
if spirits are real?" Because we attend no church and practice no
established faith I have no party line to feed him, no well-traveled
pathway to the otherworld. While I have no desire to substantiate for
Aaron a world of ghosts, gremlins, and possession neither do I want
to give him a world spiritually denuded, barren of soul and ephemeral
passion.

So I do what I must as a responsible parent; I answer a question
with a question. "But Aaron, just what do you mean by spirit?" I say

into the steam.

"Well, I mean, well, I mean," Aaron bobbles this one for a while, "Well, I mean, spirits are kind of like pictures, pictures that dance around and around," he says with the openhanded gestures that always accompany the furthest reaches of his interpretations.

And, as is so often the case with honestly questioned four-year-olds, he has captured the image with greater accuracy than a Pulitzer prize-winning penmaster: the two-dimensionality of spirits, like photographs; the appearance of substance without the substance; movement without depth. Dancing pictures—he has me in a trance.

I realize what I fear most—for Aaron and, more probably, for myself—is the mixture of these two dimensions. Humanity has long created ceremonies whose purpose is to separate the living and the dead; Davy Jones's locker is meant to keep spirits locked in. Tons of dirt are piled atop the casket to assure the lid remains closed. I am reminded of the Egyptian myth of the ka, the spiritual form of the body, which was said to live on after death and revel amid the riches within the pyramids. I am also reminded of a thousand tacky horror movies depicting grotesque fantasies assaulting the weak and vulnerable.

Back in my day we were taught that after death you proceeded directly to one celestial domain or another: Heaven, Purgatory, the dreaded Hell, or, for those interested in compromise, the cartoon-titled Limbo. Though some transfers among the celestial spheres were possible, the trip from earth to the otherworld was a one-way ride, no returns permitted. The heavenly kingdom was encased behind thick walls guarded by fearsome, sword-bearing angels, whose purpose may have been as much to keep the saved in as the damned out.

No, ghosts we don't want, but spirit, well, spirit is something of which the world is greatly in need. As I stand in the steam I am faced with a cosmic question: How do I disabuse Aaron of his belief in ghosts without turning him into a debased materialist? Establishing the discrimination between spirit and ghosts will require all the sophistry of my Jesuit education, and four-year-olds have about as much affection for sophistry as they have for spinach.

"Aaron," I begin, "let me tell you one thing. There is no such thing as ghosts. But a lot of people believe that a part of us is soul, and there's more to us than just our bodies, and part of us goes on after we're dead. Do you know what I mean?"

Aaron is now standing at the other end of the tub, hurling a small sponge at the wall. It hits the wall with a splat, hangs there for a couple of seconds, then plops down into the tub. This phenomenon constitutes his response to my metaphysical monologue.

Then the believer himself, Isaac, barged into the bathroom. "Close the door!" I shout, but first, he says, he must pee. Done, he hustles back to shut the door, pulls off his pajamas, and joins us in the shower.

Big for six, Isaac has recently begun to compete with me for water space, reminding me that more and more I must make room for him. Somewhere between the ages of four and six kids bring a silence inside their bigger bodies, a kind of new space that is filled with seriousness. Which leads me to tease him all the more.

"So, Isaac," I say by way of greeting, "I hear you're afraid of ghosts."

"No, I'm not afraid of ghosts," he says without hesitation, "I'm just scared of the ghosts in the closet." To his six-year-old mind this discrimination between the general and the specific has great meaning. He is *not* afraid of ghosts. He is merely afraid of ghosts in the closet. We maneuver about in the steam, like gentle hockey players pursuing a puck in the corner.

Finally he says, "When you were a little kid, you were afraid, weren't you?"

"Sure."

This admission opens him up. "Sometimes I dream there's this monster sitting at the end of my bed, kind of looking at me slantwise." He moves his eyes down and to the left, peering over his shoulder. "And sometimes there's two monsters, kind of chasing me, coming after me. "

I don't want to think about what this means for his two
hard-driving, ambitious parents, so I go quickly for the light side:
"And do you beat 'em up?"

"No," he says, retaining his honest shyness. "I hide."

"Sounds like a good idea when dealing with monsters." I remember
when as a nervous eight-year-old each night I would fix my gaze on a
saving light bulb left illuminated in the hallway outside my bedroom;
as long as my gaze remained attached to the light, I was safe. When
drowsiness or inattention made my eyes wander, the demonic turmoil
of the darkness overcame me, startling me awake again.

"And where do you hide?" I ask.

"In the covers. I get deep down in the covers," he responds,
confiding in me his secret of safety.

"That's good. It's good to have a safe place."

There are few things more painful to a parent than the nameless
fears that accost our loved ones. I want to sit at the end of his bed
myself, ready to throttle any gremlins with gumption enough to trifle
with my "bestest boy in all the world."

But then, maybe he would awaken for a moment to see *me*
glancing slantwise at his sleeping form and. . . . Hmmmm.

The shower done, I lift them from the tub, one by one. I gently
shake them, a little tradition we have, loosening the hold of water
and, I hope, any spirits left from the previous night. Steam floats out
the open door as, combed and shining, they rush heedlessly into the
ensuing day.

Yes, as best we can we cleanse our children of the fears we know.
We populate their worlds with beings familiar to us, but always there
is a space, a space they save and fill with their own strange stuff; and
this space, no matter how hard love may strive to make it ours, no
matter how sad we may feel at the birth, in our child, of this strange
and private world, this space is theirs alone.

CHAPTER 23
BOYS TO MEN: THE RAP OF TRUTH

Maybe it's biology. Maybe it's television. Or maybe it's our
nefarious society, corrupting children's brains with
outdated, classist, sexist stereotypes.

Or maybe it's me. Maybe it's my fault.

Maybe I get unconscious glee out of my son's sexist statements,
and maybe that's why he makes them. I don't know.

Take the other day. We're riding to town, Aaron riding shotgun,
Isaac scrunched up beside me. Isaac asks me a question.

"Dad," he says, real serious, "do you think girls can do rap?"

I sensed it was a leading, even a loaded, question. He had already
formed his opinion.

Now, the Beatles sent my soul to the sky but rap music, the
monotonous, staccato repetition of spoken lines, locks my feet to the
earth. Of course, maybe that's what it's supposed to do. Rap is about
pain and violence—very earthly concerns.

As we bounced over roads potholed from a spring thaw I asked
him, real nonjudgmental-like: "Why couldn't girls do rap?"

He gave me the answer that most preadolescents give when asked
to look inside themselves to explain what they do or say.

"I don't know," he said.

I wouldn't let him off the hook. If it is my fault he is this way,
then it's my responsibility to fix him. "What is it about girls and what
is it about rap," I asked him, "that seem strange when you put them

together?"

There was a few moments of silence. He knit his brow. I waited patiently. Well, I waited. Then he answered.

"I don't know," he said.

Aaron, as yet uncorrupted, chimed in from the shotgun seat. "You're a good interviewer," he said. "Just like those guys on television."

Maybe he was trying to be nice. Or maybe he was trying to bail out his brother. I explained that interviewing is what I do for my work; I ask questions, try to help people to talk about things. Usually, though, it doesn't work so well with my kids.

But just that morning I interviewed a young man sent over by the courts because he'd been drinking and stealing. In the course of our conversation I asked him a question I ask most boys who are sent to see me.

"When I say the word 'father' to you, who comes into your mind?"

He gave me the answer I usually get. He scrunched down a little further into his chair, then glanced up, just for a second. "No one," he said.

I guess that's what fathers do, along with screwing up stereotypes; they allow someone to come to mind when their sons and daughters are asked that question. When young boys draw a blank in response to that question, I know they are in deep trouble. Those kids know they aren't women but they also don't know how to be men, so the only sensible alternative is to destroy themselves somewhere along the road to manhood.

In their own way, that's what the rappers talk about. They talk about the chaos going on as fatherless boys try to figure out how to be men. Ice T, the rapper who recently named his first son Ice, says that a rapper just speaks his mind. A rapper speaks the truth.

Now, speaking the truth has historically been a dangerous activity. From Jesus Christ to the little girl who tells her teacher that she is being sexually abused, speaking the truth has often been followed by difficult times. That's why speaking the truth takes courage. It takes a certain disregard for oneself, for one's material comfort. Speaking the truth is life on the edge.

That's where the hook comes in: Men, throughout the millennia, have had a responsibility to serve as protectors. If there is danger to be faced, then men are supposed to face it. The violence in our society is a twisting of this male protector role, wrought by a bunch of uninitiated warrior-boys who create danger games as a means of gaining mythological status. The danger games give warrior-boys their only chance to prove themselves. Unfortunately, the judges of their success are not mature men but other warrior-boys.

Maybe rap, because it tries to speak the level truth about violence and pain, because it puts the speaker out front to take the bullet for honesty, seems like it should be a man's thing. Maybe I'm reading a little into it, but that might have been what my son meant when he said that last "I don't know."

Then he surprised me. As we pulled up to a traffic light, Isaac finally spoke.

"A girl doing rap," he said, "is like a guy doing a curtsy in a skirt."

Like most kids, he was saying a lot more than he meant, but that part's my fault. Maybe he'll know better, just like his old man, when he grows up.

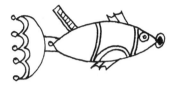

CHAPTER 24
OF GRAVITY AND GROWING UP

Most of our heavy philosophical discussions happen while we are driving around. On this night, while riding home from a nearby town, the conversation turns to the shape of the earth. Seven-year-old Isaac can understand that the earth, although it appears to be flat, is actually round. He can take himself away to an imaginary position in space and look back at his rotund home planet. He can understand that day turns to night because the earth rotates, leaving half away from the sun. But his small brow knits in perplexity as he struggles to understand why all those at the bottom of this rotating orb do not simply fall off into empty space.

Of course the answer I offer is "Gravity." But the crease between Isaac's eyes grows deeper because this is a word without reference, a word that brings no image in its wake; I might as well have said, "Schmoogleboggen. It's schmoogleboggen that keeps the people at the bottom from falling off." My response runs dangerously close to coercive faith, as in, "It's schmoogleboggen because I said it's schmoogleboggen, and your daddy wouldn't lie to you, now would he, hmmmm?"

There are plenty of appropriate opportunities to lay down the parental-coercive law: Isaac should not hit other children; he should be kind to his brothers, he should not take stuff that does not belong to him. But for the past couple of hundred years physics has fallen outside the domain of faith. It is supposed to be a science, and as I search for a suitably empirical explanation I realize I am dragging my son across centuries of human cultural development, much as I have dragged him by the hand out of crowded shopping malls or along tricky woodland trails. I am reinforcing in his mind those categories of experience that must be subjected to insistent questioning and that lead to coherent, sensible explanations. I am building a cognitive fence between this area and that of obedient faith.

Captured within his question, too, is a differentiation, a small leave-taking; no longer is the world safe because his mommy and daddy make it so. The energy in his brain drives him to stretch the bonds of the given world and through his thinking to make it his own. Whatever the quality of my responses, these dialogues must begin in the domain of parental assumptions, travel through uncertainty, and end in his discovery of himself. I know that the same energy which today impels him to understand for himself that the world is not flat will tomorrow force him—yes, this boy who only yesterday as a newborn napped on my chest—to question curfews, moral values and to in time depart to live by himself in some faraway place like Cincinnati or Mexico City or Zimbabwe.

Nonetheless, I strive to do my fatherly duty about gravity. But gravity has no metaphorical value; it is not round like a ball nor does it turn like a wheel. Gravity is like a. . . .

"Gravity is like a magnet," I venture, "Gravity holds things on the earth like a magnet holds things on itself."

"But magnets push things away too," Isaac responds, thinking of the magnet set, now mostly sucked up in the course of my callous, masculine rounds with the vacuum cleaner. "Could the earth turn around and push everything off?"

"Wheee!" cries five-year-old Aaron, tucked over by the door of the pickup truck. He has been staring out the window. He likes this part the best. "Wheee, I'm flying away!"

But Isaac is serious. He will lie in bed tonight, worrying, gnawing at his tiny nails, taking upon himself all the weight of his seniority, awaiting the moment when the earth turns round and he floats from his warm sheets off into empty space. He will struggle to return, he will grasp at empty air, but all his frantic movements will simply carry him farther away from his bed and home. This thought is terrifying.

"No, no, the earth is like a one-sided magnet. It just holds people on!" I wish, not for the first time, that I had paid more attention in my required science classes rather than believing that all science was a degradation of humankind's essentially whole-grain creative spirit. And Isaac's silence reveals his skepticism, understanding innately as he does that nothing is one-sided, not the literary-aesthetic-communitarian aspect of human existence, not the great earth-magnet.

Come to think of it, I ruminate, maybe nothing is precisely that which is one-sided . . .

Aaron turns back from the window, where his gaze has been absorbed by the play of light and darkness of the night sky, and his question invades the dim cab of the truck as a streak of heat lightning will fracture a humid evening.

"Daddy, who made all the other planets?"

Important in these situations—that is, in responding to the profound, open-ended queries posed by young minds—is offering a clear, rapid, and concise answer. I open my mouth to provide it and I realize it is not there.

Once again, effortlessly, Aaron has illuminated the boundary between faith and science; filled with conflict about the automatic answer—"God did it"—my brain kicks into gear and begins laboriously creating sense. Lulled into right-brain calmness through warm contact with my children, my awareness now switches over to the left hemisphere, searches, discovers little in the category of planet creation, rises up again over the whole brain and hangs suspended in space.

The corpus callosum carries information between the musical, pattern-recognizing, faith-loving right hemisphere and the logical, language-processing, science-loving left. I can feel its pathways glowing as I struggle to settle the war between the hemispheres and to write a peace treaty that respects the unique values of each.

"Some people," I begin in the vapid language of the left hemisphere, "believe that planets were made by the same being who created the earth, and that, they believe, is God."

"D'you believe it, Daddy?" Isaac inquires immediately in his serious seven-year-old tone. "D'you believe that God created the earth and the planets?"

Give me a break! Here I am striving to serve as a fount of wisdom and I end up, once again, cast back into the sand pit of my own ignorance. Ever since my break with the ecclesiastical certainties of my childhood I have lived with the unknown and the unknowable, I have learned to accept this hole in my faith as I accept the scars and associated weakness of my right knee or the infernal, perverse slowness of my tongue; it is something quietly acknowledged and passed over as I manage the momentary problems of living.

But now, at this moment, my children have impelled me to decide—do I believe that God created the earth and the planets? Will I declare the right hemisphere, through its emissaries and ambassadors, ruler of the left.

Yes, yes, as I pilot this well-laden pickup through the Vermont night, I do believe this to be true; that in some form or fashion a force or presence or all-pervading something which we can for the necessarily inadequate purposes of description call God was/is/will be playing a role or is in fact the role itself of the being of everything that is, the planets and the earth included. Thus, my children have forced me to an affirmation of faith.

"Yes," I state to Isaac, more conclusively than anything I have said all night. "I believe that God created the earth and the planets."

Silently I can hear Isaac's night-terror receding, I can see his estranged body lowering down through space and becoming once again warmly enshrouded within the sheets of his bed.

Arriving home, we decamp the truck and gaze up for a moment into the clear winter night. Covering myself with glory, I point out to them the one constellation I can recognize—the Little Dipper.

"Earlier tonight I saw the first star and made a wish," Isaac says, excited as always at the possible prospect of getting something new, even from the stars. "But Daddy, what would happen if you went all the way to the end of space?"

"There is no end of space," I respond immediately, as we tromp up the stairs. "Space is curved—like a wheel."

This silences Isaac until we are about to go through the door. "But what if the wheel of space flung you off, like the carousel spinning real fast at the park?"

"God only knows, Isaac," I answer, my left hemisphere again raising the white flag of unconditional surrender. "God only knows."

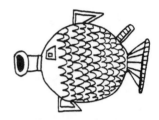

CHAPTER 25
CARDS, CLOTHES, AND THE BOOFSKER

It was the evening before Valentine's Day and Isaac was searching through the card rack at a local store. He wasn't looking at the little childish heart-shaped cards that come twenty to a box and are handed out by the millions to classmates each year. He was looking at the real grown-up cards, adorned with hearts and flowery phrases, and that was my first clue that a deep change had occurred.

He came to where I was standing by another rack and thrust a card under my nose. "What d'ya think of this one, Dad?"

I looked at the card. It was nice; raised letters, good decorations, and it came with its own crimson envelope. But there, at the end, there was talk about "love" and "my special one." Was he sure he wanted to make that kind of commitment at age ten? He hadn't even talked to her parents.

He nodded, taking it seriously. "Yeah, that's too much."

A minute later he came back with another that didn't put quite so much on the line. Then he picked out a tiny rose preserved in a plastic holder.

He had a special someone in mind, and it was making a difference. He'd cleaned his mother's car for two bucks and was spending all of it, and a little more, on stuff for his dream lady. This is a kid who, up 'til then, never saw a candy bar he didn't like and considered himself wealthy whenever he collected a significant reservoir of sweets in a brown paper bag. Two bucks still buys a lot of candy but, due to the deep change, that wasn't where his money was going.

Just the night before he had come home from a local child's birthday party all starry-eyed. "I like a girl!" he sang. He had liked girls before, but this was on a different level. He *liked* this one.

How much he cared came out the next morning as he screamed about his pants not matching his sweatshirt. This from a kid who would go to school in a torn paper bag and not even notice if the bag had old crumbs in the bottom. Suddenly these small decisions were serious. In a moment the point of life was to impress a girl and this motivated an upward aspiration and struggle for proper appearance that I knew would end only with senility.

My wife and I remembered when—it seemed like yesterday—we were staying at my mother-in-law's because we didn't have any money. Our favorite activity in those hard times was hiding in the bedroom with our almost brand new son and saying, very loudly, "Boof!"

Five-month-old Isaac would laugh and laugh and laugh a totally joyful baby's laugh that was so infectious we would say again, "Boof!" and again he would laugh and laugh as if he had never heard it before and as if he had never heard anything so funny in his whole brief life. That was about as good as it got, being broke at my mother-in-law's, and now that I remember, it wasn't so bad.

And now he was yelling about his pants and his hair and refusing, just plain refusing under any circumstances to wear the one pair of pants that happened to be clean and not torn and not too small because clearly, obviously, and suddenly it was important on this day to look like someone who knew how to dress himself.

So we worked out the first of what will be many such problems by discovering a different sweatshirt that looked good with the pants and off to school he went, clutching his card and tiny scarlet flower.

Well, that evening we learned that the great presentation hadn't gone well and now he really wished he had spent the money on candy. But I hugged him up and squished him like I love to do and told him he was wonderful and perfect and great and he squirmed and pushed me away and said, "Dad! I hate it when you do that!"

But what the hell, he'll always be the Boofsker to us, that little baby sitting on the bed and laughing and laughing like the world couldn't possibly be a better place and he couldn't possibly have been dropped out of the cosmos toward people who loved him any more, not anytime, not anywhere. And that's who we'll see, the Boofsker, even as he drives away with some future Valentine, never to be squished or schmushed again, but hopefully to continue to laugh with the same pure joy he had inside when God was good enough to give him to us.

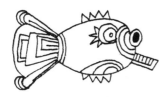

CHAPTER 26
KITCHEN TABLE BELIEFS

S uddenly, Isaac raised his head from where it was bent over a sheaf of homework papers. The overhead lamp glimmered off the liquidity of his green eyes. He turned to face where I sat shoveling down a late dinner.

"You know," he said, speaking in my direction but really intending his message for the ears of the wide world, "I'm really nervous about that play!"

It was but a few days to opening night. Isaac was playing the bad prince who sings in a deep voice and struggles to overthrow a good king and steal a beautiful maiden from the arms of the noble knight. That Isaac the Lionhearted, spiritual leader of every crew he has ever joined, could be picked for this nefarious role was not without irony. Maybe that was why he, among the range of fifth graders, had been chosen.

It made me again understand that I see Isaac as fundamentally good and pure, as deeply truth-seeking and brave. No matter what he does to disconfirm this image, no matter how often he tortures his younger brother or conveniently forgets necessary but unpleasant assignments, no display of boundlessly hedonistic appetites for candy and fun could tarnish my heartfelt visage of him as valiant and shining and noble and true.

Maybe that's what's missing from kids' lives today. There is no one to maintain the good image against all odds and from the very beginning. The powerful ancient presumption, naive in the harsh

modern world though it was fervently held for thousands of years, is
that a strong enough belief will make it so.

I remember when I was younger than Isaac is now and I was sickly
and my grandmother from Ireland sat with me at the old steel kitchen
table and told me if you believe something hard enough it will be true
and I was supposed to tell myself that I wasn't sick and eventually,
she promised, I would be well. That belief had apparently gotten her
through some tough moments on her journey from the soil of the Old
Country to a decent apartment in a city in the New World and now
she was giving it to me so that I could bring it with me on my journey
wherever I would go. In this way she let me know that believing in
yourself and in each other is both a choice and a responsibility.

I asked Isaac if he was nervous because he was afraid he would
forget his lines.

No, he answered, he knew his lines and he did not suffer from the
actor's terror of standing before a crowded room with a blank mind.
But still, he was afraid.

At this point his younger brother popped up from his own pile of
homework. He thrust an arm across his breast and assumed a posture
of maximum dramatic power.

"That is because," he said, "you are a coward!"

Isaac rolled his eyes and turned back toward me. "I don't know,"
he said, "I'm just nervous. I don't even know why."

It was that uncertain fear, the worst kind. The kind that lingers in
your stomach and reminds you during every peaceful moment that
something is wrong.

The wrongness is the key. There is a wrongness about how things
are that reveals itself to our body long before our mind hears anything
about it. Things are out of kilter, not as they should be - and because
of this incongruity we know we are at risk. Like the gazelle who
suddenly hears in the breezes of the verdant a new threat and raises its
head to listen, the wrongness says that we must stop whatever we are
doing and attend to the danger. We ignore the fear at our mortal peril.

But this was just a play, a small display before the good people of the community. And even if he stammered and croaked and fell on his face they would applaud because they were not unkind—or at least they didn't want to be thought of as unkind. Unlike nature, modern suburban audiences do not kill their losers.

No, it was situational anxiety, as the shrinks say, the heightened expectation that precedes all big events. We worry, we are afraid, because we care. The big game, the big show, the big date, all are preceded by the same fear that accompanies the test, the battle, the duel. Our guts are not great discriminators of complex phenomena. That's the reason we spend Sunday afternoons striding along great stretches of beach, thinking about our feelings.

Is this burning in the pit of your stomach a sign of grave danger, a signal to flee for your life? Or is it a harbinger of opportunity, a sign of a risk that must be taken if you are to survive and grow?

Unfortunately the two all too often look and feel the same. Not identifying the fear Isaac nonetheless believed in himself and went on stage and played his role and bowed to applause both polite and sincere. Afterward he was relieved and tired and even irritable at the postshow dinner. He slouched at the table with his head in his hands.

Even before the entrée arrived his younger brother leapt up beside the table and again slammed his small fist to his breast.

"I must say to you, Isaac," he pronounced, "that you are not a coward!"

He sat down. As usual, his older brother ignored him.

Isaac's head drooped even lower. Now was the time of emptiness, the emptiness that follows the confrontation with the fear, the directionless uncertainty that roils around in your belly like a loose barrel in the hold of a swaying ship.

It's the thrashing around that comes before comfort, before relief, before sleep. And he will make it through because he has parents who love him and so he loves himself and so he will sleep the deep sleep of children who have the knowledge of that love. He has his own courage and some wisdom offered long ago at a kitchen table by way of an old woman delivered of the hard soil of the Old Country.

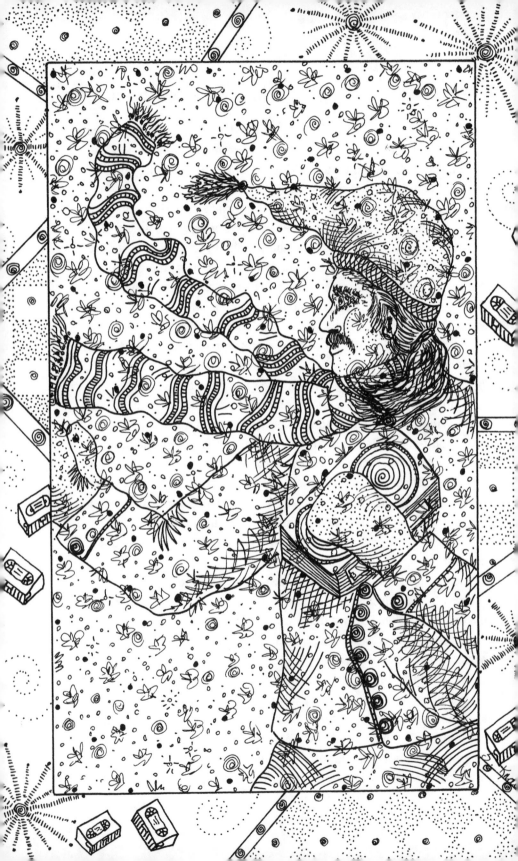

CHAPTER 27
THE BLIZZARD OF '93

The Great Blizzard of '93 found us ensconced in our
mountainside retreat, alone.

Rapidly we moved backward through time. It could have
been 1893 rather than 1993. It was dark, and the whistling wind blew
tiny piles of white snow through the door seams. Each time the gale
shifted direction the walls creaked and cracked. A quarter of a mile of
unplowed private road, covered with four-foot drifts, separated us
from a mile of unplowed dirt road, which in turn separated us from
miles of unplowed main roads.

A few hours earlier, while daylight remained, I did another of the
stupid things I am prone to do. Despite the drifting snow and whiteout
conditions, I decided to return a cassette movie to the local variety
store. My Irish soul desperately wanted to avoid the $2 charge for an
additional night. And I figured, hey, we live in a day when anyone
can get anywhere, anytime. Nature is no longer a serious
consideration.

Even worse, I completed an initial trial run down the driveway and
found it virtually impassible. The wind and snow cast my truck to the
right and left, and I backed up beside the house again, deciding that
prudence should be the better part of cheapness.

But no. Perched in the idling automobile I could not fathom that
nature had the power to prevent me from going where I will. Casting
an invective to the sky I slammed down the accelerator and hurtled
forward into a wall of whiteness.

About four hundred yards later I piled into a snowbank. I put the truck into low four-wheel drive, arrogantly figuring to power out of the drift and on down to the store to return the movie. Maybe get a couple of others, too. Pick up some snacks for the kids.

No dice. Not forward, not backward. Not backward and forward in rapid succession. Not in four-wheel-drive high and not in four-wheel-drive low. In the brief time I sat there, wheels spinning, screaming winds drifted piles of snow up around the side of the truck. I opened the door to glance at the wheels and white powder immediately covered the front seat and gathered in heaps in the crevices of the dashboard. It was hard to hold the door open until it reached a certain angle, and then the wind caught it like a kite and wanted to rip it off its hinges. By the time I succeeded in pulling it closed the cabin filled with snow.

Still hardly able to believe what was happening I clambered from the truck, pushed the door closed, and faced into the roaring wind. As I staggered forward, waving the plastic movie case in my left hand as a bronc rider will wave his hat, the wind froze the skin of my face, creating that terrible pain as when you drink something too cold. Usually I consider my face to be a thing with all the sensitivity and responsiveness of a slab of meat. But this freezing thing was a bit much, even for my side of beef.

I thought of the great northern stories of farmers who, in the middle of a blizzard, venture out to check the animals in the barn and are never seen again. LOCAL MAN LOSES LIFE TO RETURN $2 MOVIE, the headline would read. "A real moron," reads the subheading. The grieving wife, reached by rescuers after a four-hour struggle, says through her tears, "And it wasn't even that good a film!"

I turned around and blundered backward through the wind and snow, every few seconds glancing tentatively over my shoulder to follow the road. I backed into a snowbank, fell over, found myself lying on my side in the snow. Snow filled my mouth and eyes and within seconds I was a part of the drift. I clutched the movie close to my breast, thinking, "*My grandparents emigrated from Ireland for this?"*

Absurdly I thought of a woman, stranded at a bus station and interviewed for a local newscast, who shouted, "I'm a diabetic! I need my insulin!" Nature doesn't care that you didn't listen to the storm warnings. Dump your change into the candy machine, lady, and pray. About fifty percent of the time, Nature has been known to listen.

Finally I made it to the house, bursting through the basement door frozen like Warren Beatty in *McCabe and Mrs. Miller*. My face was scarlet red and felt like it had been shot full of novocaine. Had I made it half a mile down the road instead of four hundred yards, I would have gone down with my truck.

The experience made me realize how much we have all come to assume that at the other end of something, be it a road or a phone, is someone who will take care of us in a pinch, someone we can depend on. Always, *out there*, is someone who will make it right, someone who will protect us from our own stupidity, someone we can blame if things go wrong.

Nature, however, is a pluralistic despot. She warms us, fills us with sunny vitality, then sends a typhoon into the coast of India, killing two hundred thousand. She coats the trees in a spectacular, shimmering show of snow and ice, then buries your car under tons of white. But do we blame her? Do we say, "Damn Nature, let's put her in jail for good this time!" No, in Vermont, where the wind still blows huge whorls of snow up into the grey sky, we forgive Nature for her trespasses, as we turn a blind eye to the trespasses of the star athlete who is capable of carrying the whole team. We don't blame her, because . . . Well, because Nature is the one place, perhaps the last place, where we have no choice. We know in our guts that, in the long run, with nature there is no mercy, and so there is no judgement.

"Something there is that loves a wall," wrote Frost. But, if you happen to be Irish, something there is that loves banging your head against that wall, especially if it is made of snow . . .

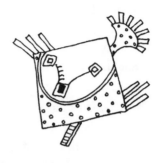

CHAPTER 28
THE BIG D

A t four years old Aaron is a New Englander born and bred, so two seconds after his eyes pop open his small feet hit the floor and soon I feel him crawling into the still-warm sheets beside me. Dragging open my uppermost eye I see his profile, no bridge to the nose as yet, holding aloft in his hands some plastic creature and holding forth with meaningful dialogue in whispered tones.

But this morning, as I am pulling on my tie in readiness for work, he puts aside his fantasy man and poses a serious question.

"Hey, Dad," he says, "we're going to live way, way, way more than ten thousand years, right?"

Even as I sleepily struggle with the third rendering of my necktie I am already faced with a serious choice; my first impulse is to respond with the Hyper-Masculine Sarcastic: "Ya, sure kid, but let me tell you the middle three thousand years go by mighty fast." This will serve to convey to my son the cold-eyed control appropriate to a man, which, after all, Aaron will be some ages hence. It will teach Aaron that death is a monster men face with the same attitude brought to all potential tragedies—pure, unvarnished denial.

Sometimes, I would be saying to him, there is a big, green, hideous, festering, putrescent scumbucket of an obscenity right in front of your face and, if you choose to be a man, you must choose to go on as if it is not even there. Yes, it's going to happen to us all, even you, beautiful little boy. If you are lucky or blessed you too will get old and rickety and die, so you might as well just go ahead and be terrified and then forget about it like a man.

But I know that he will learn not so much from what I say about death as from how I handle myself in the face of this issue—this issue called the end of our lives. Surely he will not notice that I am flopping my tie like Harpo Marx, that with one brief question he has placed me in a deep, deep trance—for, if we grown-ups do not protect our children from death, what good are we?

Should we insulate our children from the thought, from the emotional appreciation of death, as well as its actuality? Do we big-brained humanoids gain from our infernal awareness of our own finitude? If the medical-industrial complex came up with a form of psychosurgery that lasered-away the fear of death, would you truck on over to the office to set up an appointment? If they offered a two-for-one sale, would you bring your child along?

Or maybe I should share with him my own Image of the Optimal Death—I am ninety-seven years old, having lived a full life; I am walking to breakfast, newspaper in hand, on a sunny day; I am in perfect, radiant health, no problems with my colon or thyroid or pancreas or bowel or any of the other forty million inner parts whose guarantee, always of questionable legal standing, expires completely after the age of fifty. I briskly raise my knee to negotiate a curbstone and simultaneously I suffer a massive cerebrovascular accident—in other words, my brain literally explodes—and I am as dead as a stone before my foot touches pavement. I lay there in the street, amid the gathering curious crowd, with a slight smile on my deeply wrinkled face, having released my spirit in the fullness of time.

Oh, but there are other images, among them the crotchety-Irishman-dying-by-inches-in-the-hospital scenario, as part after failing part of my one and only body is surgically removed and tossed into a dumpster somewhere, there to call out to me through long pain-filled nights. Yes, to be honest there are many such scenarios, scenarios the potentiality and inevitability of which lead me to want to feed myself headfirst into the nearest chipper-shredder. No longer needed to protect my child from saber-toothed tigers, I must now protect him from saber-toothed fantasies of death.

By this time Aaron has become bored with my paralysis and has again picked up his latest petroleum-based guy; and his big brother Isaac has pulled himself from the sack and sits head in hands on the corner of the king-sized bed.

I choose a middle road—like most guys I hate to disappoint anybody, most of all my children—mollifying anxiety and yet providing a cold dose of reality: "Aaron, you could probably expect to live about one hundred years—and that's a long, long time."

I don't tell him that he doesn't have way more than ten thousand years, a mere one one-hundredth of ten thousand years is all he's got—can he see the end already? Won't he, shouldn't he live for a while in the blissful delusion of immortality, the belief that life is an endless expanse spreading out before him with time to piss away on idle twirling around in the backyard or flopped on his back tossing a ball at the ceiling or pulling open the refrigerator door for the hundredth time, gazing in as if at some beneficent deity?

"But Dad." Aaron gestures with two open hands. "I don't understand this. What happens to you when you're not alive any more?"

Big brother Isaac lifts his head from his hands and takes this one into his fogbound brain: "Part of you goes away somewhere else while another part of you stays here and gets buried or something." He twists up the side of his face in uncertainty. "Part of you goes and part of you sort of stays but doesn't really . . . oh, I don't understand!" And he returns his face to his hands.

The cold clarity of Aaron's four-year-old logic leaps forth: "What part of you? Where do you go?"

Isaac's head jerks back up; he mumbles, "The part of you that's not your body . . . goes somewhere . . . "

Now Aaron screws up his face in a manner genetically similar to his brother: "My body?" he says questioningly, "Part of my body is not my body?"

For Aaron to know his body he must know that part of him is not his body, he must comprehend where his body ends and the rest of himself begins, and this he does not know; as a matter of fact, if he understood that there was something about him which is not his body, he could answer his own questions about life—in a manner consistent with the way our culture divides life from the body. And I could finally tie my tie, get these guys dressed and fed, and get myself to work, where I handle paper and people according to clear rules accepted by all concerned.

"Well," I say, seeking to sum things up in a neat package. "Some people believe that when your life is over your energy, your self, goes back to the universe, goes back with everything else. Then people have different ideas about what happens from there."

"My energy? My self?" Aaron shakes his head; I can practically hear him muttering: What a bunch of nonsense.

My eyes travel then to Isaac, whose big body still sits on the corner of the bed; he's just recently grown too large to carry around easily, as I used to love to do—or maybe I've grown too old.

And then I notice that he is quietly crying.

Tie still awry, I go to him and put my arm around his small shoulders. "What's going on, guy? What's happening?"

His head droops; tears drip from the rims of his clear green eyes down to the carpet. "I don't know."

"C'mon, tell me," I say, giving his shoulders a squeeze. "C'mon."

There is silence for a moment; then he looks up at me with glistening eyes.

"What happens to the trees after they fall down? What happens to the bushes and the little animals?"

His head drooped down again. "I didn't know life was going to be like this," he said.

That, I swear on whatever sense of universal unity you choose to experience as sacred, is what he said, just like that. "I didn't know life was going to be like this." As if, from his perspective of six years, if he had his druthers he'd just as soon go back and forget the whole thing. There he had been, doing just fine inside his happy, healthy mother, and now this: animals and trees, dead.

Needless to say, this tore me up a bit. Again I was failing at protecting my children from inevitable realities. Aaron was playing at combat with his plastic guy, but it was Isaac who was caught in the existential crossfire. Proof positive that a lot happens between the ages of four and six.

Well, Isaac, my dearest son, to be honest with you, I didn't know life was going to be like this either.

"And what happens to the stars?" he went on with rising hysteria. "How did they get there? And why are they so far away? And what happens when they disappear?" The tears were still flowing and the voice was becoming ever more alarmed. "What happens? *What happens?*"

I was no less chagrined; all my typical masculine logical responses were worse than useless, but I had to do something. I could yell at him, tell him to stop being so sensitive and perceptive and human, order him to get tough and out of touch. I struggled to discern a response of a different order.

"Isaac, close your eyes."

"Why?"

"Just close your eyes. Please." Reluctantly he squeezes his damp lids together. "Do you see the lights back there?" He shuts his eyes more firmly, grimacing. "Do you see the different colored lights flickering?"

He nods his head, staring hard behind his eyelids.

"That's where the stars go—they go inside you, and you can see them anytime you close your eyes. So they're outside and they're inside all the time."

In a moment Isaac's face changes, relaxes, and his eyes open. He takes a deep breath and rubs his face and looks at me. Sometimes God gives you an answer. "Hey, Dad," he says evenly, "can I go play Nintendo now?"

I gave a brief laugh and looked over at Aaron. He looked up from his play.

"Dad," he says, "we definitely won't live a million year." He looked back down at his guy and glanced back up at me again. "But maybe if we exercise . . . , " he mused.

Susanna Hepburn Kadwell

CHAPTER 29
WHERE IS THE KING?

W hy is there rampant violence in the streets and homes of
America?
For one reason.

The king has fallen.

The king is now regarded as a corrupt, stupid lummox. Any image
of a male "authority figure"—that is, of an older man who has taken
responsibility for somehow supporting the integrity of his
community—is presented in the media with mockery and sarcasm.
From The Simpsons to President Clinton to Louis Farakhan, male
figures of respect are torn apart in a frenzy of humiliation.

Male figures are first degraded within the community and then
expelled from the family. As everyone knows, more than half our
marriages end in divorce. In 97 percent of those cases, custody of
children is awarded to the mother. A year after divorce, a tiny
minority of fathers see their children more than once a week. In
addition, a million children per year are born to single mothers. In
this way, more than two million children per year are rendered
fatherless.

In a decade, that comes to twenty million people, roughly ten
million of them male, raised without fathers.

Ten million men, raised without the consistent presence of an older
man, ten million armed with weapons of violence, trained by a
degraded media to practice violence, urged to use intoxicating

substances to feel powerful, and thrust from the home into a dangerous world before they have experienced the presence of a father.

They are the army of unfathered men, and, all around the world, more and more of them are marching into battle.

But they don't fight in the service of the king. They don't struggle to serve the values defined by the king, values that he has in turn learned from God. Instead, they serve the value of momentary impulse, or the values of unfathered men little older than themselves, or the values they saw demonstrated on last night's television movie. But they don't serve the king. They hate the king.

For the king has fallen.

And now, the army of ten million unfathered men is loosed upon the land.

For centuries, every unstable civilization has been defined by this characteristic: a huge group of disenfranchised, isolated, socially disconnected men, destabilizing the ship of state as they rush to and fro, supporting everything from fascism to anarchy.

The Germany of the past. The Somalia, the Serbo-Croatia of the present. The America of the near future.

But we may well ask.

Why did the king fall?

The king fell for many reasons, not the least of which was his own greed and ambition, his turning away from his sacred responsibility and substituting instead a life of self-indulgence. But then—and now—no one *wanted* to support the king. Most people feel that the king, simply because he is powerful, must be defeated.

We have become very good at defeating kings. We have become so good at defeating kings that very few men of value will even attempt to become kings. Worthy men know that to stand up before others, these days, is to suffer being thrown down, to be thrown down and have your mouth stuffed with dirt.

King, sure. Some king!

There was a time—only a few short moments ago in evolutionary time and for hundreds of thousands of years—when families were the center of life. In families, children were taught how to survive, how to worship what was sacred in the world, how to treat others with compassion.

Men were a part of those families. Fathers were a part of those families.

Men and fathers were a part of the process by which sacred information was transmitted from person to person, from generation to generation.

No more. Now men, and fathers, are regarded with contempt. Many people, including many men, believe the world would be better off without them.

Many men are suicidal in this way, feeling, as they reel around the world, that they are of no value to others. And then they must believe that they are of no value to themselves.

So what difference does it make? In the absence of any tradition, where does a man get his sense of purpose? Where is a boy to learn his sense of purpose?

A boy learns his sense of purpose from his father.

A boy learns a sense of purpose from a father who, for some moments in his young life, the boy must hold in his heart as king.

But, as we said earlier, the king has fallen.

The king is dead.

Long live the king!

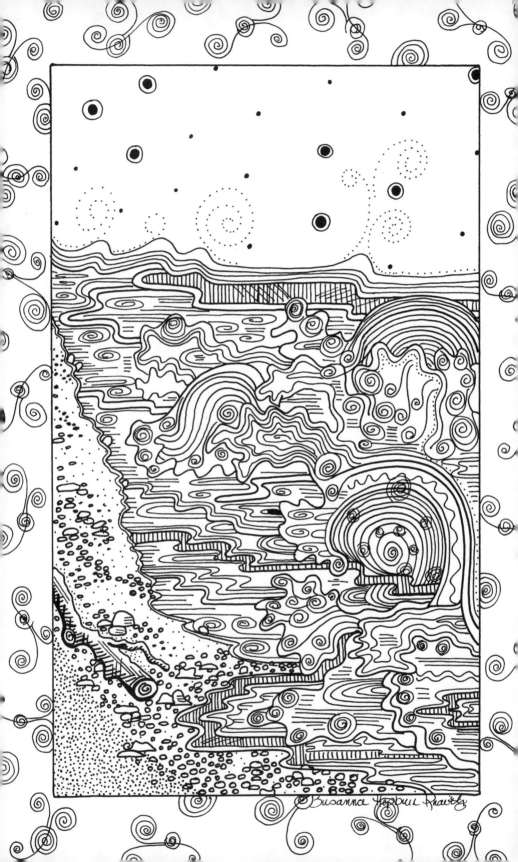

©Busanna Hopbule Knowles

CHAPTER 30
THE HEALING SWORD

Off to one side the waves crashed repeatedly, washing onto the dark sand and then retreating with a rattling sound over the millions of small stones lining the beach.

It was an overcast day and close to the water a fine salt mist filled the air. The beach was a narrow strip at high tide. The wind and waves roiled up toward a short concrete retaining wall.

Aaron and I were on a mission to find wood; wood suitable for whittling. Wood that is going to be whittled, that is going to have some innate, internal character revealed through long patient labor, must have some character to begin with. And wood that has ridden in the sea for hundreds and perhaps thousands of miles, wood that has been taken by weather and force and crazy circumstance from some far place and thrust into some other place where it lies alone, pale and twisted, has character in every dark line and knothole.

Aaron Malachi bent down and picked up a piece of driftwood from among the stones and sand and hefted it in his small hand, turning it this way and that to determine if it had the required magic. Then he turned his freckled, sun-drenched face to me and said, over the roar of the waves and wind: "Swordwood!"

He extended his arm and scrutinized the length of wood in his hand, venturing a couple of practice thrusts, eyeing the wood all the while as an expert horseman might observe a stallion being run around a ring. He was putting the wood through its paces to see if it extended his power; imagining himself using it to slay all manner of dragons, gargoyles, and monsters.

Yes, I could hear him thinking, yes, this swordwood will serve me well to guard the boundaries of myself. It will help me defend my six-year-old spirit from the powerful intruders who threaten to take away what precious little freedom I have.

And with two bigger, stronger brothers he has need of all the power he can get. It is not by chance or fantasy that every stick is whittled to a sharp point and that point is then directed outward toward whatever force would mock a child's strength. These same forces, he fears, might tear him from his home, cast him upon the wide sea, and let him drift to a strange place where he would wash up, tumbling forward in the turmoil of a wave to lie exhausted and spent in the sun.

You reach for that which has been cast out for protection from the power of that same place; a son reaches out to his father, the father to the grandfather, the grandfather to God, Y*W*H, Allah, Krishna, Buddha. Only that which has ridden on the sea can protect a boy on his first voyage; can turn his weakness to strength and his innocence to wisdom.

Aaron reached out and felt the heft in his hand and imagined the waves and the miles it has traveled and he thought, yes, with this I can persevere.

For thousands of years the carrying of a knife or a sword did not mean you were off to kill your neighbor. To be armed did not carry with it the present implication, "armed and dangerous"—the image of a mad and malice-filled man prepared to slay whatever crosses his path. To be armed merely meant that one carried in one's hands or at one's side the means to protect oneself. To be armed was to enforce peace within the boundaries of the self, thereby creating the conditions for the evolution of an inner life.

Now there is no swordwood and every child can possess a machine for killing, a machine that was not conveyed by an elder, a machine that has not ridden on the sea and so taken on the sea's wisdom and depth. The machine makes a loud noise and leaves a great mess behind and can be used at a great distance, all characteristics that appeal to children and to adults who feel empty and afraid. The machine that kills messily and loudly and from a great distance is a tragic caricature of being armed, and the latest drive-by shooting is invariably perpetrated by children who have been violated, degraded, and disarmed and is much ado about the nothing they feel inside.

Such children and vacant adults kill because they have no way to connect to the wisdom and power of the years, no way to gain from the collective pain of the generations that preceded them. They have no swordwood.

Aaron and I examined a huge gray log that the power of the sea thrust up onto the beach. Its surface, dark and shining with saltwater, was smooth as wet marble. Here and there the stump of a branch protruded, snapped off at the base during tumultuous travels. What remained was only that which was seaworthy; there were no extras, no frills, no doodads. It was a bare log, worn clean by time and experience.

"I'd like to see you pick that one up!" Aaron yelled through the roar of the breakers.

I just laughed. "That's swordwood for a giant!" I yelled. As for you and me, little one, we'll continue our search for the sword that protects and heals.

CHAPTER 31
OF ANTS, IDENTITY AND
MIDSUMMER AFTERNOONS

It was a midsummer Sunday afternoon and I lay on the couch in a deep drowse watching a procession of ants march up a damp tree outside our living room window. The bark of the tree was grayish tan with deep fissures, and the ants were pure black, their plump hindquarters shining in the dull light.

Though, in terms of ant vision, these ants must have been far out of sight of one another, somehow they followed a precisely similar path through the deep valleys and crests of the bark. As they demonstrated this incredible feat of remote coordination, no ant audiences applauded their acumen and no ant cameramen filmed their achievement for future generations of ants. They climbed up the bark with the terrible silent decisiveness of all purely natural behavior, and it is only ant psychologists who would ever know if they regretted their anonymity.

But the impatient voice of Aaron, my eight-year-old son, roused me from my ruminations. "Dad, let's *do* something!"

I didn't take my eyes off the ants. "Do you want to play cards?" Cards was something you did at the beach on dreary days; you sat around a table and played gin rummy or pitch or poker and you quietly passed hours in which neither work nor active play was possible.

"No," he said as he leaned forward on the other couch. "Let's go bowling."

There was a long gap in the procession of ants. Surely the next one would be confused, would fall with a terrible ant scream from the bark of the tree.

"Let's do something that doesn't cost money," I said, though my own torpor issued a strong internal objection. "Let's *do* something, not *buy* something."

"But everything good costs money," Aaron hastened to observe.

I turned away from the window and looked at him. "Being loved by somebody and loving somebody is free, and that's the best thing."

As I heard myself saying this, I was aware that I might sound like a hectoring parent; but sometimes it's a father's job to lob one out there.

Aaron responded quickly. "Paula and Jason are getting married, and that's costing them a lot of money," he said, referring to an aunt who was at that moment planning a big wedding bash.

I almost said that it was the wedding, the ceremony, that was expensive; the love was free. But I sensed if I said that I would create in his young soul a polarizing differentiation between love and marriage, between feeling and action, between mind and body. And, as we all know, love and marriage are already polarized enough. I didn't want Aaron to think that marriage is a container that confines the freedom of love, but that is the way it would sound, because those are the differences that men have believed in and fought for. Aaron's insistent questioning was forever getting me hung up on these dilemmas, forcing me to choose between what was and what I wanted him to believe.

"Anyway, the love is free," I said, avoiding the issue. "How about if we go kayaking?"

"No."

"You never want to go kayaking," I said, continuing in the lecturing mode. "If you only do the things you think you want to do, then you never get surprised, you know, when you find out you really like something you didn't think you'd like."

Aaron shrugged. "It's not a good day. It's all wet."

I laughed. "But kayaking happens on the water. It's supposed to be wet. Why don't you want to go?"

Aaron was silent for a moment. He spoke then in a mocking tone, like a robot, "I-do-not-know-the-answer-to-your-question."

"You don't know why you don't want to go kayaking?"

There was another long moment of silence. I thought that he might be changing his mind when he finally said, "Yes."

"Yes, what?"

"Yes, I don't know why I don't want to go kayaking."

"Well," I came back, "I sure don't know why you don't know why you don't want to go kayaking. I don't even know why you *do* know why you don't know why you don't want to go kayaking, if you know what I mean."

It was Aaron's turn to laugh. "I can't help it. I just don't know why I don't know why I don't want to go kayaking."

It looked like we were stuck in one of those loops. I turned away to look out the window and noticed that the ants were gone; probably back in their ant living rooms, drinking little glasses of ant tea as they discussed the efforts of the day. My adult self insisted that people should know why they do things, and therefore by extension should know why they didn't do things. I remembered when I was a small child my mother would hold me on her knee and listen while I asked her "Why?" and "Why?" and "Why?" again to every statement she made. She was patient and tolerant and even seemed to enjoy it. In reality, because she maintained a home for five children in addition to working full-time, she probably did it about twice in my life, but it was enough to keep me asking, here, forty years later.

"So what do you want to do that's free?"

"I want to go play basketball," he answered.

"But the courts are wet."

"So what? I don't care."

"Now, do you know why you would rather play basketball than go kayaking?"

"Basketball is exercise," he said.

"So is kayaking," I rejoined.

"And it's competition."

So that was it. Drifting on a bay, observing the birds cutting through the gray sky and the wind as it subtlely altered the surface of the water, all that lacked a competitive edge, gave no adrenaline surge. Aesthetic experience was not a game that could be won or lost, with a score that told you how you were doing along the way. Children are threatened by the lack of structure involved in pure aesthetic appreciation, and so they revel in the clarity of the score, the organizing possibility of victory.

And our media, oriented to the eight-year-old mind, play and prey upon this hunger for organization through competition. If a human experience can be rendered competitive, American media will film it and sell it. Kayaking itself, a wonderful way to glide through the water and observe the world, was a "sport" practiced with enormous energy by competition addicts the world over. In the sport of kayaking, you measured your miles in minutes, and your awareness was as internally focused as if you were running on a treadmill. In this way, the American media machine is slowly converting millennia of human experience into one grand vacant game of competition.

Outside I noticed a single black ant making its way up the tree. It moved back and forth in a frenzied manner, and its movements were more nervous than its predecessors. It was as if the trail was cold and this lonely ant now strived to recover any smell, any sign, of its long departed compatriots. Was this the lazy ant, the one that had refused to be roused from its ant bed when the call for traveling came? And was it now experiencing the desperate, natural consequences of self-indulgence?

Or was this the ant, ostracized from the group because its antennae were too long or too short or too straight or too curly, who now, like all irrevocably different creatures, must find its own way in the world?

That was the wonderful thing about ants; their courageous and generous anonymity allowed you to impose upon them the story of your choice.

"So no kayaking?" I said, giving it one last chance.

Aaron shook his head, arms folded to reinforce his position, "Uh-uh."

I grunted and raised myself up to a roughly vertical position. "Okay, go get the basketball."

As Aaron ran from the room I took one last glance out the window. The lone ant was far up the tree now, hardly visible, but still moving, still searching.

And that's the thing that's different about kids; if they're strong and healthy they won't let you impose upon them the story of your choice. They'll fight like devils to make up their own story, their own too curly, too straight, too long or too short story.

And that, for better and worse, makes all the difference.

CHAPTER 32
TOO MANY KISSES

It is a scene familiar to millions of American families: Three minutes remain before you all must get in the car and go somewhere—anywhere—and, using your voice alone, you must impel many small bodies to perform the ten thousand rituals which precede departure. Your voice rises in volume as it is again and again proven that your children possess entirely separate nervous systems and are capable of completely independent action, 'til you find yourself screaming monosyllables from some old 1960's absurdist one-act play, as in "Socks!" "Face!" and "Time!"

One recent afternoon my wife was delivering just such a soliloquy whose purpose was to impel our Isaac and Aaron up the center staircase. "Now!" she orated. "Shoes! Bathroom!" Isaac ascended each step with the alacrity of a man twenty times his age. Suddenly—if you can describe the interruption of something that is hardly even happening as sudden—he turned back toward his mother.

"Wait!" he shouted plaintively. "First I want to give you a kiss!"

My wife was not fooled by this old ploy. "That's the problem around here!" she shouted in response to his request. "There's too much kissing and not enough listening!"

From where I stood by the door, bags drooping from my rapidly tiring hands, it took a few seconds for the true wisdom of her remark to set in. It was one of those events that emerge from the boundless flotsam of daily life, like finding a beautiful red fire truck among the anonymous pile of broken plastic that children's toys inevitably become, or like hitchhiking along a superhighway and discovering among the roadside debris a diamond ring that someone threw out their car window during an argument. You pick it up and scrutinize it closely, wondering skeptically if it can really be as valuable as it appears.

I realized that this one stridently voiced statement expressed all that afflicts our family, indeed, all that afflicts Western civilization. Too much kissing, not enough listening!

I thought of the French, who kiss each other two, no, three times upon each encounter or leave-taking. That is entirely too much kissing, without even considering the nefarious French part. Do we see the Japanese grabbing each other's faces each time they encounter each other on the street?

And as for listening! I remember when, as a young boy, a guest would come to our house and I would sit raptly listening to his discourse for hours. Indeed, I don't believe I spoke a word until, at age sixteen, I asked for another piece of meat loaf, and even then no one noticed. In those days, children were not to be heard and, if possible, not seen either.

I don't know about you, but it seems to me that children talk a great deal more than they did in years past. Long ago, it seemed that conversations between adults and children were both tedious and, usually, fruitless. Children listened to adults for the minimum requisite time and then got away as quickly as possible. And even the thought of a kiss evoked excruciating embarrassment.

Now we shower our children with affection and listen to their every word in the hope that they will grow up to be psychologically secure adults, with good self-esteem. And instead they do turn out to be people who talk a lot and like to be kissed a great deal. Meanwhile, the trade deficit grows, and in our high schools kids spend their time talking and smooching.

As my wife wrestled our younger son to the ground to tie his shoe, I realized how desperately we need to reverse this alarming trend.

More listening, less kissing! That's what America needs! Or, maybe, parents need to do a little less listening and a lot more kissing.

At that moment five-year-old Aaron Malachi hurtled down the stairs, taking the last three at a leap. He stood there, legs spread wide, red cap with an "A" on the front forced down atop his protruding ears, a cardboard sword dangling from his tiny fist.

"Eeeehah!" he screamed. "I'm gonna hot wire your soul!"

"Car!" I shouted in response. "Lunch! Soon!"

"Window!" Aaron called out, dashing past me.

"Life!" shouted my wife.

And so, after a few kisses, off we went.

CHAPTER 33
TO READ OR WRESTLE

It may be a mystery to some people why the verbal development of girls significantly exceeds that of boys, but it's no mystery to me. Night after night, as I prepare to put Isaac and Aaron to bed, they proclaim they would rather wrestle than read.

"C'mon Dad! Just for a little while up on the big mattress! C'mon! C'mon!" Isaac is dragging me by the wrist up the stairs, though upstairs is also where they would lie quietly in their beds as I read to them. He twists my arm slightly as he pleads, as if some subtle initiation of the wrestling process will support his argument. Which, of course, it does.

"Yeah, yeah, yeah!" shouts Aaron, jumping up and down and flapping his arms. "Let's wrestle!"

I am torn. Fathers reading to children, and being read to by children, is an essential aspect of development and teaches the power of language, the magic of imagination, the ancient intimate campfire ritual of shared storytelling. The long moments in a dim bedroom as a human voice defines another tale of conflict, adventure, and resolution, prove that words are not only a woman's ally, but can also be befriended by a man—for at least a little while.

But wrestling; the contact, grappling of skin against skin, squealing, leaping, impact of body upon body, the long, slow descent of a towering form to the mattress, where it impacts with a soft thud and is pummeled frantically by the gathered force of small people. Is this something other than language? Does wrestling exist in a domain separate from words? Does the dance and dodge and sudden strain of wrestling live in a primordial place separated by impermeable lace curtains from the sacred hall of language?

Not too much convincing is required to induce a bunch of guys to choose wrestling over reading, and maybe that's the problem. Increased testosterone levels lead males to choose physically exciting activities over intellectually challenging ones and over many years the cumulative effect of thousands of such choices has consequences, transporting men to Mars and women to Venus.

But having enough testosterone left to be easily tempted, I let myself be guided in the direction of physical encounter.

I knelt on the mattress while the boys bounced in their bare feet. Isaac was now tall enough to meet me eye to eye this way, and I no more than doubled his weight.

They used a variety of grunts and smacks immortalized over years of televised pro wrestling shows, and I used the physical armor developed over years of contact sports. Men may innately know, or certainly learn over time, how to tilt a head to soften the impact of an incoming blow; how to raise an arm; tuck the chin; curl a shoulder down to create a protective barrier; how to shield the soft and vulnerable parts while sustaining the brief sting of contact; how to follow a body's momentum and bring it down; how to pick it up where it bends and turn it over in the air without hurting it; how to move one's mass while depositing only a fraction of it on the other, increasing or lessening that fraction in relation to the mass of the other.

These are skills in movement that men have known since time immemorial but now only practice in sports, when making love, or when wrestling with the kids, unfortunately in that order.

In these wrestling bouts a child feels the father's strength and his restraint, his power and his self-control. The child's joy in wrestling is also his satisfaction in taking these attributes into himself.

An episode of wrestling frequently involves tears, negotiation and renegotiation of rules, banishment and summary exile to a separate space, forgiveness and reengagement. No, Aaron may not hit Isaac in the face with his fist; yes, Aaron must spend five minutes off the mattress for his offense; yes, he may then return and join in the fracas in blessed forgetfulness. And that rule includes hitting with the open hand as well and with sneakers and with books. Rules are negotiated, enforced, sustained; another five minutes off the mattress; tears, banishment, forgiveness.

Our family for one will say that wrestling no less than reading is essential for healthy development. The learning there is equal to that in a hundred fairy tales.

And besides, when else does a father get to lovingly hurl bodies like so many sacks of grain and have it yield such happiness?

Susanna Hepburn Kravitz

CHAPTER 34
THE BREATH

Early Saturday morning the phone rang. I dragged myself out of bed, scooped up the receiver and felt that little bit of excitement, mixed with anxiety, that comes whenever the phone announces its presence or I pull down the lid of the mailbox. It might be an invitation, a check, a message from a long-lost friend. More probably it is a bill or a notice to the occupant that a new charge card can be had if only I will believe a modest pack of lies.

But this was a call for my son Isaac. Isaac wasn't home and it was my job to inform the caller of his whereabouts. Information received, the caller hung up and pursued Isaac elsewhere.

That's pretty much the way it is these days. The phone rings, someone is looking for Isaac, and Isaac is off somewhere, doing something. I have a mental image of where he is and what he's doing but that's all happening in my mind. My immediate senses are involved with something other than Isaac. My experience with Isaac is more and more secretarial and abstract in this way, with an occasional transient sighting, a familiar flash in my peripheral visual field.

There was a time, seems like yesterday, when no one called for Isaac and he was usually right there beside me, pulling at my ear or sticking his finger in my belly or just leaning back, relaxing, with his head tucked securely beneath my chin.

It was at these moments that his smell really got to me. I'd put my nose in his hair and breath deep an aroma that rushed to my brain and elicited a million years of unthought lineage, eons of wandering across vacant windswept spaces, centuries of gazing out at unknown vistas with a hand resting without thought on the shoulder of him or her whom you would gladly give your life to protect. It all came back as I breathed in the centuries and squeezed his small belly and tucked my nose in the small space behind his ear.

Now, when I thought of it, when I thought of the intensity and the passion of attachment to my Isaac and his present newfound distance from me, I wanted to sink my face in a pillow and sob . . . well, sob like a child. They say that the child is father to the man; maybe he's father as well to the child in himself.

It is this contact, this inhalation of the deep essence of kindred spirit, that has become eroticized in our desperate media-mad culture. Many's the time I've patted my child on the butt and wondered what the human service police would make of such a gesture. The tickling, the wrestling, the kissing and nibbling of neck and belly and shoulder, any one of these, in particular when performed by a man—a father—could send the shrill tax-supported monitors of propriety scurrying to a phone so that the child could be removed from his home and sent to a proper State facility where he would be raped by an authorized employee of the Department.

Feeling the small abrupt shape of a collarbone, drawing a finger along the fine line of an infant chin, we are so deluged with erotica that any loving contact, particularly from a man—a father—is a sign of lust. In this way the most primal bonds are crushed and distance becomes the proper mode of the day.

But by luck and some animal impetuousness I had breathed deep of Isaac. I'd changed a thousand diapers, given him a hundred baths, roused him from his perfect slumber at midnight and watched him stand in a trance in the dim light as he pee-ed into a toilet for the first time. In all these moments I'd had my chance to breath him in, and now, now he was out of my sight and Lord knows if he would ever come back.

Now, I have to admit, every once in a while I can restrain myself no longer and I grab him as he rushes past and I squeeze him tightly and take a good snort of his hair. But now his squirmings have an edge of real anger—he has better things to do than play with his father.

It is the kind of pain that mothers have dealt with alone in our industrialized world, this pulling away of the source of life and hope and joy, this little death that is a precursor of the Big Death. If a father now chooses to breathe in the Life he takes in with that numinous substance, the inevitability of loss, and the pain and joy, as the cosmos would have it, are always of at least equal measure.

Sitting alone on the couch I hang up the phone and look back over the long years of hugs and squeezes, the ease of joy and laughter, and tears rim my eyes. They well up and up but they do not fall; they do not fall because I am hopelessly a man, a man condemned to keep his space inside even unto the moment of loss.

So this one day I breathe deep the Isaac-less air, sigh a sigh of Isaac-less resignation and turn away into what's left of my own life; and I cannot help but wonder, were I to create a monument for all the ages, how it could ever compare to the deep unity of a single breath.

CHAPTER 35
FATHERING THE DREAM

A s I stepped from the elevator into the vacant hallway, sound from the big-screen TV rushed to fill the dayroom of the Old Soldier's Home. Glancing reflexively to my left, I saw Curtis Strange's near life-size form lining up a thirty-foot putt. The white sphere rolled slowly across a smooth expanse of grass and approached the dark void of the hole. As the ball spun the roar of a crowd in a sunny Hawaiian vale rose like a wave gathering for shore, flowed through quadraphonic stereo speakers and washed over the old men scattered throughout the room. Most of the men sat unresponsive, staring at the floor or out a window or down into a cold cup of coffee, and this wave, generated by a golfer eight thousand miles away, caressed them. The ball rimmed the hole and the collected voices crashed suddenly down onto firm green lawns these men would never see.

None of the men in the dayroom, I saw, was my father. I wandered down the hall toward the nurses' station and found him there, strapped into a special rolling chair. In front, the chair had a little expanse of tan desk. I went over and noticed how the skin sank in from my father's prominent cheekbones; the same skin I, as a young boy, had rubbed with my face as I thrilled to the harsh prickliness of his beard.

Now he sat staring at the bare expanse of imitation wood before him, head tilted slightly downward, hands gripping the metal connecting poles with all the remaining strength of his body. Nodding to the nurses I went to him, said hello into his unresponsive face, unstrapped him from the chair. With my supporting hand firmly planted in his far armpit we set off down the hallway.

I thought as we walked that my children had never known this man, my father, when he radiated strength and life. I took them dutifully to this hospital over the long years of his deterioration and they patted his hand and my older son, the extrovert, even gave him a hug. But they had never seen him standing before the steps of his house in the old neighborhood, the house he bought for $10,000 and rebuilt from the ground up, as the men of the community gathered round him in respect.

You could tell from the tone of their voices, those other men, that my father figured high in their esteem. For he had done what all of them had set out to do: Without money or education he had, brick by brick through his own determination and strength, built himself a life. And just the way he stood there, with a foot resting casually on the bottommost step, you had the feeling he might yet do much more.

So all those men wanted to be on his side; they knew that now or then he might tell them how to put a toilet in a basement or get a job at the U.S. Post Office. He'd come up from the ground and so was connected to it, and they knew that behind him, in the ground, was the power they would never challenge.

No, my sons had never seen him standing there in his glory, they'd only seen him when through some strange chemistry of generations he had chosen not to do more, had chosen instead to retire early on the products of a hard youth and spend the dwindling days of his life in desperate misery. Having somehow stepped away from the parabola of his life each day he flailed about for some connection, some rope to stop his precipitous fall. He was terribly uncomfortable in his comfort, and at the heart of every lazy day was a silent scream.

That, unfortunately, was the part my sons saw. They even had for him a special name: "Grumpy Grampa." He was at best avoided, at worst tolerated. His intelligence and his strength no longer justified his prominent faults: his stubbornness, his reticence, his threats of violence. No longer needed by them, the fawning friends fell away and he was left on a lonely, isolated island. It wasn't a graceful decline. Ornery Irishman that he was, he was not going gentle into that good night.

I gently but firmly guided my father around a table in the dayroom. On the huge TV screen the shining golden locks of Greg Norman flickered in the breeze as he positioned himself over a drive. With the camera following, the ball cruised through flawless blue sky.

I positioned my father before a window and pointed out to where the hospital lawns, and beyond them the long stretch of the superhighway, extended off into unknown distance. I remembered a year earlier, before the disease had got too far along, I took him out to lunch at a local restaurant where he ordered three desserts and an understanding waitress indulged his eccentricities. Having dipped a long spoon deep into a sundae, he stopped suddenly and leaned across the table. His face grew serious. "I've decided to rejoin the Navy," he said. In this way his frazzled brain reached back for the days of glory, days when he appeared at the door clad in brilliant dress whites, freshly returned from adventures in Manila or Tokyo or North Africa. I looked into his eyes and wished that it could be true.

Now for a moment as he gazed, his face came alive, intensity returned to his green eyes and his whispering lips moved slowly in some silent, personal language. Turning from him I too looked out and, yes, there it was—the world.

Then his eyes retreated and with his right hand he reached down and fondled the firm wood of the windowsill. He used to love to talk about wood: yellow pine, cedar, and precious cherry. He'd built from scratch an ornate hutch standing still in my mother's living room. Back when we were kids we wondered what it was about wood, what difference it made if it was hard or soft, and what it was about it that made it better than plastic or metal. The subtlety of wood too, and its complex vulnerability, was for him just another area of loneliness.

I remembered how he would tell us, by way of affirming the value of education, that he could have been an engineer, a mathematician, a professional. Like Marlon Brando in *On the Waterfront* he could have been, but for his responsibilities - but for the five of us. At 28, an age when I was finally getting around to pursuing doctoral studies, he had already been to war and back, gotten married, had four children, bought, remodeled, and sold a double-decker house. He chose to sacrifice his dream to a certain kind of work, and the pain of his loss contaminated the idea of sacrifice for his children and affirmed, oh yes, it affirmed the inestimable value of a dream.

For he knew how to work. Yes, he knew how to haul like a horse in harness, but he was sweating, cursing proof that labor without love, that work without the vitalizing energy of a dream, is death.

I guided him past a series of tables, past two men who stared at a checkerboard cleaved by a lance of sunlight, past a low Formica table adorned with a fan of unopened magazines to the hallway. Behind me, as I glanced back, a pale sphere dropped from the sky and bounced on a smooth green, once, twice, then lay still.

I sat my father back in his chair, snapped the straps and inserted in their proper slots the poles of the imprisoning desk. I brushed my hand over his pale scalp, feeling the remaining warmth and the smooth thin strands of his hair. I told him, in a whisper, that I loved him, as I had never told him when he was younger and more conscious because I was too angry, too angry and too unaware of the simplicity of things. I whispered that I loved him and turned away and walked past the nurses' station and down the hallway to the elevator. Then I looked back and saw him sitting there, small and bowed against the pale tile wall. The elevator door opened and I heard from the dayroom a long, sustained cheer, and my last backward glance revealed a dark-haired man raising an iron shaft to the sky as the sun illuminated his ecstatic face. Then the door slid closed and I silently thanked my father for his paradoxical gift—the gift of a chance to dream.

CHAPTER 36
WHY IT MATTERS

I was rushing to change after work when Aaron stopped me at the top of the stairs.

"Dad," he said, touching my forearm, "Does the past matter?"

I froze, one foot on the landing, the other on the step.

Yes, I thought, that's really what he said. He said, *Does the past matter?*

It's not a question one expects to have to consider in the hectic hour after returning home. A father's mind is on mundane concerns: homework, housework, soccer practice, dinner. Perhaps there is a hopeful projection of a blissful future: the newspaper, a snack, some television, and then, perhaps, rapturous silence.

And the question, once introduced into existence by Aaron, had a shimmering quality that meant it could not be ignored.

Does the past matter?

I thought my way down the steps, unbuttoning my shirt, as he followed. Part of me wanted to say that the past doesn't matter, the past is gone and to be constrained by the past is to sacrifice the vitality of your life to shadows and chimeras. Great cruelty comes from allowing the past to matter. People from Haiti to Bosnia are torturing others because the past matters to them. Forget the past. Forgive the past. Don't let the diseases of the dead contaminate the moment you have now.

But in the end the past is all we have of our lives. It is the source of tradition, community cohesion, time-tested love. It forms our identity, our reputation, our legacy.

In a moment I made one of the countless decisions defining our role as parents. Though my free spirit yearned to voice the former opinion—"Does the past matter? Nahhh!"—my sense of responsibility impelled me toward the latter. A parent's first job, it seems, is to teach his children about duty, about truth and integrity. Someone has to err on the side of ensuring that future people understand what they are expected to do even if they choose not to do it. It ain't always easy or fun but, somehow, it seems right.

Parents too get sick of worrying about what's right. Parents, particularly fathers, want to do what they want, want to step out onto the path of adventure, of pleasure and freedom. They want to take down the stop sign, forget the past, and roll free and easy on into the future.

But, hey, so what?

Since the speed of light vastly exceeds the speed of typing, all this passed through my mind in about an eighth of a second.

"Of course the past matters," I answered.

I sat on a chair untying a shoe and we looked at each other eye to eye. I could see the thoughts swirling in Aaron's head like smoke curling over the surface of a pond. "It's the only way people know anything about you."

He looked down. I knew then that this had more to do with confession than philosophy. A better question might have been: Do you want the past to matter? Indeed, does the past matter whether we want it to or not?

"Well then," he said, "I have something to tell you." His body got all squirmy as kids' bodies will when they have something hard to say. "It's about something I did."

What he did will remain confidential, but it was the kind of thing kids do when they're not doing what they know they're supposed to do. It was a little thing, but wasn't right, and he knew it, and if the past mattered it had to be said.

I congratulated him for saying it even though it was hard, and then we talked about what he could do to make it right. I realized then what we do with kids is to try and get them to develop in such a way that the bad feeling they get when they do something wrong will outweigh whatever advantage they have gained in doing it. As parents we try to influence this balance in the direction of conscience, which is nothing other than realizing that the past does matter, and if we fail at this task we consign our children, and others involved with them, to lives of confusion and pain.

Children learn that the past matters because they see their parents acting as if it does. They see adults working hard to make the present bear some sensible relation to the past, to make the present grow from the past or make amends for the past or improve on the past. And children realize if the past matters they matter, because in addition to being a bundle of present needs for candy and bicycles and sneakers and movies, children are also in the process of becoming personalities, of becoming human.

And they seem to know, or if they don't they need to learn, that a person is nothing more than a past with a chance; one more chance to look back into the shadows, and then ahead, and step hopefully into a present that matters.

Susanna Hepburn Knavity

CHAPTER 37
THE GREAT TOY MAKER

A thing both great and difficult about kids is that they raise deep, complex theological questions that often get postponed until after dinner, after football practice, after music lessons, after work, after tomorrow.

But kids won't have it. When they've reached what the Catholic Church used to call "the age of reason"—seven or eight or nine—questions bubble up from their incessantly boiling minds. The questions must be asked. And answered.

Time spent alone with a child facilitates the questioning process. Also, I've noticed, these questions often emerge in the bridge-time of early evening, as deepening shadows portend the close of another day.

And frequently they are brought on in the dim enclosed space of a truck's cab. For one thing, pickup trucks don't yet have televisions. And the radio's speakers have been bounced to tatters so they remain silent.

As we bounce along a dirt road a question surfaces in Aaron's mind and emerges from his mouth—a mouth that now has two huge front teeth bursting through a previously vacant gum line.

"Dad," he says out of the jolting silence. "Do you sometimes feel like you're a toy for God?"

What?

What should I say? Sometimes I feel like a sunrise over the ocean, sometimes like yesterday's trash. But a toy for God? Well . . .

"It's not that I feel like a toy like one of my toys," he goes on, "but it's like, well, we made the toys and God made us."

I get the message that he does not want me to think this is a childish discourse about toys.

But he wants me to understand that he understands this analogy, so similar to a question on the Scholastic Aptitude Test: "People are to toys as God is to . . . "

The universe? The Grand Canyon? Me? All of the above?

"Sometimes I think," Aaron goes on, waving his small hands in the dusk, "sometimes I feel like I'm just here, and it's weird. Not scary or anything. It just feels weird to be here—like I'm a toy for God."

When Aaron's older brother Isaac was a baby, I would carry him around town in a backpack and we would cross a bridge with the cold river running underneath and he would peer down over the concrete barrier and bounce up and down in the backpack and squeal, "Too deep! Too deep!"

I wonder if this God and weirdness and toy stuff is like that. Too deep.

What he may have come upon is the fundamental, startling, evanescent realization that, due to an improbable combination of circumstances including biology, evolution—and God—an amazing event has occurred—he exists.

The realization may have crept up on him as he lay in bed, eyes wide open, head resting on his pillow.

How about that? I am!

I ask him, where does all this deep thinking come from?

He says, "Well, I've been thinking about this more since you've been reading us the Bible."

His mother, a nonpracticing but profoundly affected Jew, and I, a nonpracticing but profoundly affected Catholic, were bothered by the potential effects of our nonpractice on our children. Figuring everyone needs to understand the Bible, I started "in the beginning."

Genesis was exciting. So much happening so fast! Creation, contentment, shame. And then the flood: a wrathful God, goodness surviving against evil in a closely contested struggle. And Cain and

Abel—what better story for two battling brothers to hear? Where does it come from? Not from the source of childish toys.

"You know," he goes on, "it's good that you feel shame, because then you know that you did something wrong and you can do better."

This must be the Catholic part talking. Back in the fifties we were taught that shame was something to be proud of. Only good people felt shame, so getting people to feel shameful was an essential part of getting them to be good. Thus the famous words, drummed into us at every opportunity—"You should be ashamed of yourself!"—were both condemnation and praise.

These are the kinds of mysteries and paradoxes understood only in the mind of The Great Toy Maker. These are the subtleties and conundrums encountered by little boys and girls who, having for the moment left toys behind, suddenly find themselves on the brink of reason and wonder.

Of course, the wonder of presence also brings with it some anxieties, which then call forth patience and fortitude.

"I know I don't believe in hell," he says as we pull up to the house, "And I don't know if I believe in heaven." He turns to look at me as he wraps his tiny fingers around the door handle. "I guess I'll just have to wait 'til I die to find out."

To find out if he is, indeed, a toy for God.

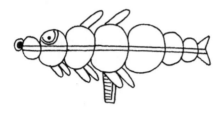

CHAPTER 38
HOW IT WAS WITH THE HAT

A seam formed in the milling mall crowd and ten-year-old Isaac burst through. In his right hand, I saw, he was holding something.

When he reached me, we stood still, creating a small island around which the crowd parted and flowed as it passed. He raised up what he had in his hand. It was a cap.

"I want to get this for Eric's party!" he shouted above the din. He had been invited to a party that afternoon at the house of a friend.

I looked at the cap. It was a florid orange color, with a long bill, and over the projection of the outsized bill was printed in bold green letters, "Mine's longer than yours!"

I experienced a sinking feeling. How could Isaac, my son and blood, choose such a tacky gift? I glanced toward him and wondered. I asked him, in a voice a little hoarse with the effort of shouting, "Do you know what they're talking about when they say it's longer?"

We were being jostled more as we stood still among the passing throng. Soon we were going to have to move, or we would be swept away.

Isaac's bright green eyes looked into mine. As he looked the light of dawn rose in his eyes and the muscles of his face slackened. Then he grimaced and raised his palm to his forehead in the universal sign of surprise and chagrin.

"Oh, no!" he said, coloring now. "I thought they meant the bill of the cap!" I could hardly hear him in the banging, shouting maelstrom.

Running through the din was the constant roar of ten thousand collected voices. Isaac snatched the hat from my hands, turned away, and dove into the crowd.

Abandoning my post I walked on, pleased that at least one ten-year-old still fails to understand that every expression of innuendo must refer to the sexual wherewithal of the male or female. The sincerity, the naiveté, the capacity for surprise is charming and is probably the main reason why, in this media-saturated world, we love children.

The problem with knowledge, of caps or sexual innuendo, is that once you know something you can't ever not know it again. Once you are of a certain age and you begin to think about alcohol and drugs and cars and sex then everything from that point on will remind you of it and there is no way, no way at all, that you can get back to being the person you were before you became the person you now have become.

Years ago, I guess, a tree was a tree and an orange was an orange and a river was a river. Every once in a while some poet would say a lady's eyes were like diamonds or her breasts were like apples or her hips were like the broad side of a barn. But then the Victorians came and covered up the table legs and tried to suppress every prurient metaphor and then it all exploded so that today you can't look at a set of lug wrenches without thinking about beer and sex.

So the time before cultural detritus overwhelms a child's brain is a precious time. These are sacred moments when he or she looks out at the world and sees it for what it is, nothing more or less. And you want to preserve for your children that time when they look to you with questioning eyes and ask you to tell them what things mean from the mountain of garbage inside your own brain, and you do translate it, carefully and conservatively, because you want to keep them from having to go to that mountain of dross, or the mountain from coming to them, for as long as you can. So, around eight or nine or ten or eleven they don't know what's going on and you don't want them to know what's going on because once they do they never won't know what's going on again and then they'll be involved in the great idiotic race and next thing you know they're walking in the door with a little bundle of joy for you to worry about for the rest of your life.

So you hold on to those moments, the precious moments when the wall of unconscious purity still stands before the onrushing sea of petty knowledge, moments when the bill of a cap is still the bill of a cap and you can hand your friend a gift that doesn't mean anything more than what it is.

Because it's when things stop being what they are that they start being more or less than they are, and then the world starts slipping away and we can see the hands of time whirling and the sun crashing down into the West and the world turning, turning, turning and we want to protect our children from this inexorable march, the same march we find ourselves well out on, so far out that we can see the end and when we do see the end we only wish that we had appreciated it more, had valued it more, when we were, like them, at the beginning.

So I tried to go a little slower than the rest of the people at the mall, to saunter along and notice the faces and the clothes and the way the light, even the bright, merciless florescent mall light, brought people out into the world and how they changed from moment to moment. And up ahead I saw my precious Isaac leaning over a counter gazing down at tie clips and wallets and cuff links and I wanted to run up and put my hands on his cheeks and gaze into his wide green eyes and tell him, tell him just what he needs to know right now about how things change but I knew it wouldn't make any difference, he'd just look at me like I'm wacky and tell me to cut it out and ask me if I like this tie clip and then he'd continue charging down his road, shining as he goes, gleaming pure and bright like we all do, and did, in the beginning.

CHAPTER 39
AARON'S THIGH

It was a sunny spring day and my wife and I were debating the family consequences of her pursuit of another college degree: who would *really* shoulder the burden of time spent in the classroom and on the road to the university; how would the lost income be replaced; and where would I live, goddammit, if I wanted, finally, to have a life of my own?

What was fair, what was right, what was sensible, and whose job is it, anyway, to take on the responsibility of understanding the other's dreams and really feeling the other's fantasy of self-fulfillment? Whose task is it to look deep into the eyes of the other and see reflected there the two-headed dragon of excitement and desperation?

The kids tumbled into my truck to be driven to school as we stood on the deck exchanging final declarations. Each of us wanted to please the other *and* ourselves and we had to choose, for our own small drama, between the roles of martyr and hero. The concrete fact that school begins at a precise time lent some structure to our fervent strategizing and we ended without resolution.

At the school I leapt from the truck so the kids could slide across the seat and out the door, giving each lad a kiss as he passed. As Aaron hopped his bottom across the seat I placed my hand on his tiny chest and stopped him.

Set off against the pale flesh on the inside of his left thigh was some brown stuff—two lumps and a couple of thin rivulets trending down.

"What's that?" I asked, pointing.

He looked down at his upper leg, then back up at me. "I don't know." He shrugged his small shoulders. His clear green eyes shone with honesty.

I gently massaged one of the lumps with my right index finger. It was soft and it extended in a line from where his shorts ended but it had about it a luminosity that was reassuring. I raised my finger to my nose; any chance of identifying it by smell was swept away in the morning breeze. Some ancient instinctual sense suggested, though, that shit don't shine. Such discharge, in my experience, is generally unreflective, absorbing the light as it does the toxins of the body, creating an opaque lump. But there are exceptions.

Still gazing at his pale thigh, Aaron reached down a pudgy finger and without hesitation wiped it through the mysterious substance. He then inserted the laden finger into his mouth. His eyes raised up to meet mine as his tongue worked the finger over. There was a serious, perplexed look in his eyes as he lowered his hand. Finally, he rendered his verdict. "It's okay, Daddy," he said in his soft, reassuring tone, "I think its chocolate."

He wiped the remainder of the brown stuff off his thigh with the heel of his hand and schmushed it onto the front of his shorts. He kissed me on the cheek, leapt from the truck, and was swallowed into the playground crowd.

Driving the rest of the way into work I was bothered by the thought that something very profound had just occurred but I could not discern its meaning or sense. I had the firm belief that this momentary interaction about the brown stuff revealed everything about childhood and adulthood, about mystery and risk, about the joyous tragedy of time's passing. This moment was one of those moments that had contained within it the kernel of every other moment, all time glowing softly like the glimmering brown veneer of whatever-it-was.

It said everything, for example, about how we approach the unknown. Timorously had I touched the suspect stuff, held aloft the affected finger, peered cross-eyed as I positioned it a safe distance from my nostrils. My sudden shock at apprehending the brown mystery was accentuated by Aaron's decisive movement in sampling the strange substance. I had felt some anxiety, but also, to my shame, some relief, that this boy, my son, was going to research this question. Was this the first of many times I would rely on him to take a risk I fear?

Yes, that was it—the mystery, and my withdrawal in the face of mystery, and his advance. That's what it was, this dance of generations, the coming forward, the falling back, humans circling each other as we will, taking in our wonder or holding it away—is it a sign that my time is already past?

Is it time for me to watch his courage, to take a seat in admiration and applause? This caution, this grown-up caution, it has infected me with fear of brown stuff and every other sort of strangeness that comes my way. Having been burned my share, I pull away from every mystery as from a hot stove, and finally every sense of warmth I scrutinize with a hard eye. Yes, yes, it is time for me to sit and watch and acknowledge that he can now do what my old youth has left undone.

So there is sadness here, and joy and wonder too, at his balance, his wondrous calm, his certainty of tomorrow still intact—that is what brought his finger down and up again. Thus ensconced beside time's headwaters undeterred his caring flows into each moment's tributary, then flows right on, no swirling around in gathering pools, twisting down to depths the same as surface. Is deeper better or just a way of making well the cowardice of those of us who wait?

These were the questions that came as I pondered the brown stuff, and what came along with it. Here we had, on his pudgy leg, the heartland of the human struggle: is it shit or is it candy? As we approach each moment, can we ever know? And youth will learn before age, will do the right research to find both the bitter and the sweet. And I, I will watch and read from my secondary place.

Yes, that was it, the sugar and the shit, we can never know which it will be and we must draw very close if we are to learn the difference. Age, without thinking, trembles at this closing, strains its ancient eyes to see from afar, whereas youth accepts the deal as is, and so age grows tired while youth grows wise.

When I arrived at work I phoned my wife to let her know that I would support her in her schooling, in making real this part of her dream. I mentioned that the brown stuff told me, told me my questioning would never cease and that before life can be judged it must be tasted. I think she understood. I think she sensed better than I could say that we must act before we know and forego resolution for participation, and, oh no, don't thank me, I said, interrupting her—thank Aaron's thigh.

Susanna Hepburn Knailtz

CHAPTER 42
FATHER AND SUN

It was one of those kitchen table existential nausea moments; questions invaded an area of peaceful domesticity and sent it spinning down, down, down into a depthless void.

We were at breakfast. Cereal boxes, arrayed about the table, stood like so many 2001 obelisks. Metal spoons clanked in porcelain bowls. In the air were the quiet slurping sounds and gentle nodding motions of feeding children.

Four-year-old son Aaron, spoon held aloft above his half-emptied bowl, opened his mouth—not to eat, but to speak.

"Dad," he said, with a distracted air, as if asking for the funnies or the sugar bowl. "Will you die or will the sun go out first?"

I was blindsided.

These questions used to make me feel like I'd been thrust into a 1930s movie with Claude Rains, back when the drops fell gently on shining Parisian sidewalks and wind made the candle flicker but not go out and I could be filled with existential grief without feeling too awfully bad about it.

But not now: Now, with the children gathered round the table and me staring at life from midway; now, when deep questions of life and death seem messengers from quieter, wealthier times; now, when my energy is sharp-tuned to care about what happens in the next ten seconds, or at most ten minutes, not the next ten years or ten billion years.

Of course I knew the answer to his question as, most likely, did
he. It's just that he might have hoped it could be different—as, most
surely, did I. When I was a young man pacing slowly down a familiar
avenue beside a friend I once turned to him and said, with all
seriousness, "I'm never going to die!"

At that moment I believed it. The young blood raced through my
veins like a swollen river. It roared and twisted over its rocky course.
It covered the stones and overran its banks. The infinitesimal moment
of time that was mine stretched out toward curves beyond which I
could not see, and, like all children, I took my space for the horizons
of the world.

But now, now with the aches of yesterday's adventures creeping
into my joints, I knew it wasn't true. I would die, yes, and yes, some
time thereafter the sun surely would go out.

But wait; for a while now the son still goes round the father as the
earth circles the still-warm sun. He, my son, is still centered here at
this table, even in this moment of knowing that there is something
beyond himself, beyond his father, beyond the mighty all-providing
sun.

I know that within his four-year-old mind he is elaborating with
care the permanence, and impermanence, of things. I could tell him
that, with luck, I will live until I am old and he will live far beyond
when I am old. But the sun; no, I will not witness its demise, and
neither will he. When its fury collapses into a dense black hole or
surges forth into a red giant, our fevered contribution to this universe
will long have disappeared into unfathomable time. He will
understand, he must understand, here at the brief beginning of his life,
that there are endings and there is The End. And the task of ever-
youthful imagination is directly proportional to the power of the
ending it must overcome.

Perhaps, ten billion years hence at the moment of the sun's demise,
all consciousness will exist in some disembodied pool that needs
neither light nor heat to carry on. Perhaps we will cruise like strange
eagles through the layered vastness of the universe.

Or, perhaps, there will be no more than silence.

It is this last option from which we shield our young. We fight with all the power of mythology and faith to craft a following chapter that encompasses this end as part of a larger story, so that story consumes story as day consumes day. Will we come, ten billion stories hence, to a narrative so large, so vast and unencompassable that none further can be imagined or believed?

In short, are all our stories of sons and suns ecstatically exploded in the name of God? Or do they extend in a long, long line that, far beyond the curve that stops our vision, quietly and irreversibly ends?

To these questions we can only answer: Who can say?

But, in our moments of courage or commitment, we do say. We say to our young in our various symbolisms that we are part of something that even the end of the sun cannot extinguish. We hold a child's face in our trembling hands and we say these words of faith, filled with a parent's terrible earnest, urgent, pulsing desire, not to save ourselves, for we have seen enough to accept the inevitable end, but to breathe, yes, to breathe into those we love a chance for life.

Yes, that's true, I could say, your old father will not outlast the sun. But, dear Aaron, who can say? You and I, we may believe a story that transports us beyond the sun, to a place too large and too full to be encompassed by our mere breakfast minds—to a place where hope and faith are one.

Who can say?

Susanna Hepburn Kravitz

CHAPTER 41
AHH, SURRENDAH!

Aaron is at the stage when fantasy works; he gathers unto himself various multicolored pieces of plastic and begins a whispered conversation among them. Though he carefully protects the privacy of his domain, if I discreetly lean close I can just discern exclamatory phrases among the hubbub: "Fly away together!" "Band together and attack!" "I'm the strongest in the world!" and the like. He will occasionally spend a full thirty minutes in such solitary play, moving his guys around on the table or floor, stepping back now and then to admire a guy in a particularly fetching or combative pose.

I am flattered—and a bit shaken—when Aaron invites me into his world.

"Dad," he says, "Will you play with my guys with me?" And when I accept it is with a mixture of pleasure and trepidation—the feelings I have when faced with doing something I might enjoy but about which I know nothing.

Aaron, assuming the identity of a guy who looks like a punk rocker version of G.I. Joe, defers to me in his play: "What do you want to do?" his guy asks my guy.

"Let's go to Texas!" I suggest impulsively, "We'll have to fly there!"

Simultaneously, our guys develop miraculous powers of flight and levitate from one end of the peeling picnic table to the other.

"Na weyer in Texas, so ya hafta tak lak theyus," one guy says to the other upon landing. We set out to explore the territory.

Then Aaron, as stage manager, introduces more characters into the drama; there are the bad guys, with drooping mustaches and dark hair—not unlike his real-life Dad, come to think of it—or else huge, impersonal robot-creatures. They are brought into the game for the single purpose of being eliminated, but when I express an oldster's reluctance to pull the trigger, Aaron responds, "But they're just bad guys!"

Resolutely I hold to my temerity; straightening the arms of my guy with some difficulty and extending his hands over his head, I approach one of the bad guys.

"Ah surrendah!" I insist.

For a moment Aaron, now speaking for the bad guys, is confused. "You can't surrender! I'll kill you if you surrender!"

"No, no, you can't kill someone who surrenders," my guy says with great urgency, "That would be dishonorable. You've got to protect anyone who surrenders to you. So, I repeat, ah surrendah!"

Then we went about surrendering to any and all available opponents: robots, aliens, hot rods—Aaron approaches a daisy which has popped up through our trampled lawn: "I surrender!" he declares to its drooping petals.

With surrender comes an end to conflict—and how dominant a master can a daisy be? Soon we have declared our peaceful intent to all nearby forms of life, and with practice we seem ever more strongly protected by the mantle of surrender. It was this way, I can remember, in the old schoolyard; there invariably was a kid—usually the smartest in the class—who could not be beaten because he would not fight. He just said (a bit enigmatically, to be sure), "I know you're tougher than me, so what's the point?" The bully spouted threats for a while, but like a wind without a sail he blew himself out in time; he knew he had been vanquished by stoic surrender and his promises of doom became a pointless, humiliating stage play, one that even he could not carry on for long.

Clad in this paradoxical armor Aaron and I explored the world beyond the picnic table, beyond the maple tree, beyond even the high stone wall, observing and befriending all we saw there. We asked the hedge about itself, tracked an ant in its purposeful journey. There were those whose names we knew and those we left unnamed.

"What is this?" one asked. "Why, I don't know," the other responded, and we left it at that and stared in wonder. Some strange sort of thing, it just stood there waving, not asking anything of anyone, or so it seemed. And on we went.

As we traveled I learned (and maybe Aaron learned, too, though I must admit he already had the more natural gift) that to pretend is to dream, and to dream is to surrender—and with surrender the world opens itself and shows the strange and wondrous meanings we can't see as we work to make it fit our myriad plans.

As two miniature men work their way through three-inch grass the world unfolds itself anew, and we shared that brilliant, unhinged sensation one has when approaching an old familiar neighborhood from a different direction, and for a moment, the moment before it all falls back together, the familiar is entirely strange. Four-year-olds are masters of this reorientation, and as we train their febrile minds to defeat the foreign threat in the battle of computer science, we had better remember to help them hold onto this dreaming thing as well.

We went across the world this way, with our mantle of surrender working to protect us, save for once when a knee was skinned while clambering over rocks. Some time was spent in grieving but miraculous powers of healing prevailed, and on we went, this time directed like the ant toward home.

Safely returned we savored our voyage, leaning our guys back in repose. Aaron, feeling incomplete, begged to shoot at something, if just to hear himself say "Bang!" a time or two. Not being able to deny his pleading eyes—and needing now and then even to surrender our surrender—we expended a few fantasy rounds at the picture of a bull adorning my coffee cup. He seemed satisfied.

For as no life, we learned, can live without surrender, no life can change without conflict. But that's another story.

CHAPTER 42
THE MEANING OF MASCULINE DRIVE

Deep questions come out of the dreary Vermont morning, as clouds hang low in the distant valley and wispy swirls of white slowly ascend the mountainside. Five-year-old Aaron and I sit alone at the kitchen table, solemnly spooning cereal into our respective mouths as we gaze wordlessly down into our bowls.

Without warning Aaron breaks the silence, turning his head toward me as the question leaps from his lips.

"Daddy," he says, out of the morning stillness, "What are pork rinds?"

Now, this is one of those inquiries which does not allow obfuscation: Either you know what a pork rind is, or you don't—and I don't. Though I live in the country, split wood in autumn, take in buckets of maple sap in spring, tend vegetables in summer, and in winter—well, during winter I sit, moderately depressed, in front of the television set with my children and play Nintendo. Tennis is my game. I have reached Level Five and won an imaginary $50,000.

"Would you please be quiet!" I have been known to yell at my kids as they bounce around the living room during a particularly tense point in a match, just as John McEnroe would upbraid the fans at Wimbledon or Flushing Meadows. They are not yet old enough to understand that there are few moments in life when fifty thousand imaginary dollars ride on the push of a button.

But as I, like Freud, have studied my own psychological

development (before Freud, spending years studying yourself was known as damn selfishness, but since has attained the stature of a science), I have come to realize that these imaginary Nintendo dollars are nearly as important to me as the real dollars that pass through my checking account with blinding speed. As a matter of fact, I probably garner more real satisfaction from the fifty thousand imaginary Nintendo dollars than I do from the meager amount that is weekly electronically channeled from my automatic deposit account to the debtor of the moment.

Which makes sense, considering the first is an electronic/imaginary gain and the second is an electronic/imaginary loss. And we wonder why children become addicted to Nintendo.

Back to pork rinds. As Aaron eyed me expectantly across the kitchen table, I was filled with the familiar feeling fathers have when their children present them with questions about which they know nothing. This experience is significantly different than it is for mothers. A mother would say: "Gee, Aaron, I have no idea what a pork rind is! Let's go over to the encyclopedia and look it up together!"

Whereas a father will say: "Well, uh, uh, a pork rind is a rindy sort of thing that comes from a pig. Hey, aren't you ready for school yet?"

"But Dad," Aaron would say, "I don't have school today."

"So what!" a father would reply. "You should be prepared for the future! Always remember that."

Philosophers of the Far East have long asserted the basic PHILOSOPHY OF THE FAR EAST, and that is, in short: Everything has something to do with everything else. So now the question is, what do the difficulties of discussing pork rinds have to do with excellence at Nintendo tennis?

Well, those Far Eastern philosophers are right, at least as far as they go. Because it is the same impulse that makes it so difficult for fathers to simply answer "I don't know," when asked about pork rinds that makes men good at things like Nintendo tennis. It's the masculine drive to be right, to be perfect, to be powerful. Men care deeply about Nintendo tennis, just as they care deeply about having the right answer about pork rinds. So deeply, in fact, that in the absence of the right answer any old answer will do. Having an answer is equated with winning, and for men, winning is everything.

So pork rinds and Nintendo tennis go together like soup and nuts, like America and indebtedness, like yin and yang.

Now if I can just convince Aaron to go outside to wait for an imaginary bus so I can skim a few minutes to practice my unstoppable serve . . .

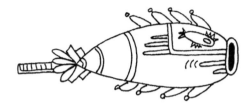

CHAPTER 43
CHASING THE DREAM

It was an unnaturally warm spring day and I was about to dash out for a little conditioning run.

As I squatted on the floor tugging on knotted tendons, the phone rang. I crawled over and scooped it up.

"Hello, is Isaac there?" Isaac and his mother and brother were out shopping. Also along was a friend of Isaac's named John who, it seems, has been living in my son's bedroom since we moved into the house.

"No," I said. "He's out."

"Oh," the boy said. There was a lot of disappointment in that "Oh," and after it there was a lot of silence.

"Well, who's this?" I asked after a while.

"This is his friend, Leroy!" He said the words with a formality that most eleven year olds can't muster. And he said more than that, too. He said he was an eleven-year-old boy who has spent his whole holiday at home by himself and who thought he was Isaac's friend, who wanted to be Isaac's friend, and he is more than a little hurt that Isaac had gone about his life without him.

"I'll let him know you called," I said, and went to hang up.

"Okay," I heard the sad voice say before the receiver hit the rack.

As I went out huffing across the muddy lawns I remembered as a little boy I used to flop around the house like Leroy, now and again picking up the phone to call someone who I hoped would want to spend some time with me. I remember my nervousness, the fluttering in my tiny stomach, as I laboriously jammed pudgy fingers into the dial of an old rotary phone.

Frequently the little boy I called was somewhere else, doing something else that sounded a lot more exciting than flopping around the house with me. And he was doing it with relatives or friends, people he cared about and who cared about him; normal people—as opposed to the wayward weirdo I felt myself to be.

After years and years of childish attempts to be normal and to be accepted as normal I finally gave up and took refuge in books; at first science fiction and then Nietzsche and Sartre and Marx and Hesse. I built an armor of information around myself until I existed, it seemed, solely in the domain of literary media and was accessible only through the printed word, so that anyone who actually said anything to me in the "real" world was greeted with the kind of bemused perplexity with which an alien might greet a surprise visit by an earthling.

After reading for a long time I began to practice the art of social isolation, purposefully sitting alone at a table in the crowded, boisterous high school lunchroom so I could be fully engaged in the struggle to quiet my self-conscious mind. I ran and ran and lifted weights and wrestled to harden the soft edge of my human vulnerability as I hardened my abdomen through countless sit-ups. I worked to perfect a kind of conscious maneuver of narrowing and hardening and rising up, rising up above any real or merely perceived social mockery and allowing myself to care for neither approval nor disdain. I went out in the solitary cold and, rather than bang on the door and call out to reenter, I chose to pull my collar up about my neck and walk away.

Now, so many years later, I struggled across an open field, arms and legs methodically churning; as I ran I remembered that after a particularly embarrassing moment in early grade school I sat down and tried to hide my head inside my little desk, to crawl right into the tiny spaces between the books and papers, and I thought I couldn't wait 'til I grew up so that I could feel nothing, so I could be

absolutely hard and unemotional like some movie hero who didn't
need anyone and would never allow himself to need anyone. I
couldn't wait to grow up because as a child I couldn't help but need
people. I had no choice but to admit that I was vulnerable and would
die without the attention of others, and I absolutely hated that
coercion, the way that children are thrust onto the earth and have no
choice but to have no choice and are forced to struggle through all
those moments of needing someone and hating to need them because it
appears that those others also hate to be needed and so you know it
would be better for all concerned if you just went out the door, just
went out the door and walked away for good, but, dammit, you're
nine years old so you can't.

I came to the midpoint of my run, staggered to a stop, and
continued walking along the shoreline. Most of the houses were
deserted now except for one where a Volvo was parked outside and a
big tan dog barked at the gray sky. The sun shone yellow across the
bay and looking down off the pier the water was clear all the way to
the bottom. Down there in the green distance dark patches of seaweed
swayed back and forth in gentle motion. It took a while to catch my
breath and I swore for the ten thousandth time that I would never
smoke another cigarette, that I would practice yoga and go to bed
early and only think thoughts that are conducive to world peace. Then
I slowly trotted back up the hill.

It was as a high school senior, as I got a little bigger and became a
little handsome and experienced some athletic success, that I learned
all social contact doesn't have to be painful. People approached me
and I ran away only about three quarters of the time, and the other
quarter I struggled to communicate with certain people about the
books I had read and the thoughts I had thought and the dreams—well,
the dreams I wouldn't be ready to talk about for a long time.

Having tasted the sweet nectar of social intimacy I wanted more
nectar and I chased it with all the fury with which I had previously
pursued the dream. I ran around and around and around, the years
went by, and now there I was, sucking wind as my soles pounded the

hard pavement.

It seemed that with the loss of social isolation I had also lost the connection to my dreams. I lost the unwavering Spartan commitment that never allows itself to take into account anything but the factors of the dream. As I gained a little social acceptance I had begun to care about the things that people generally care about and with that I became distracted from the dream and so I lost the dream and the fruits of the dream and even the wonderful fruits of the valiant pursuit of the dream. In a funny way the loneliness and self-denial that accompanied the isolation, which were a direct result of my shame and loss and my consequent struggle to harden myself to the pain, were the core motivating energy for any kind of achievement, and I had to get back to that isolation, the isolation and loneliness I knew so well as a child, if I were to nurture into being any of the remaining fragments of my dream.

That has taken a long time and remains woefully incomplete, I thought as I labored up my driveway, sucking air down a windpipe that seemed as narrow as a sideways dime. Yes, it had taken a long time for me to return to the necessary isolation and maybe my own kids wouldn't have to do it that way and maybe Leroy wouldn't have to do it that way either. That might be a good thing, if you believe that suffering isn't a good thing—or maybe, maybe the suffering involved in following the dream is a big part of what makes the dream worthwhile.

Susanna Hepburn Knavitz

CHAPTER 44
PRECIOUS

The piercing sound of the baby's cry invades the edges of your sleep; listlessly you swing your feet out of bed and shuffle automaton-like to the baby's room. You gaze down into the crib in the soft glow of the night-light and there he is, lying on his back, arms and legs stretching and unstretching, eyes pressed tightly shut as the cries effortlessly escape his open mouth.

You reach down and scoop up his fifteen-odd pounds, turning him carefully so his head rests securely in the space between your neck and shoulder. You worry that maybe you're spoiling him, picking him up like this, but then they say you can't spoil a baby before a year and a half; and as he snuggles there, pressing his tiny knees against your chest, it's hard to believe that anything this warm could be unhealthy.

And then you begin The March, back and forth from one end of the room to the other, smoothing the turns so his head doesn't get jostled, feeling satisfaction as he becomes calm and quiet and slips back into sleep. Maybe you gingerly shift him over to the other shoulder as your back begins to ache a bit.

And you think that not too long ago men didn't do this kind of thing. The warm and cuddly part was left to mothers—part of the reward for having to do all the work. But now this 3:00 A.M. baby-bearing has entered the male domain, it's a job for big hairy guys who four hours later will be driving trucks and pushing steel, or rushing from the house with hair half-brushed and tie askew, getting by on five hours sleep one more time. Maybe you don't have the luxury of Organizing Everything Perfectly Around The Job, maybe you'll have to make do with the best of the energy that's left, maybe you'll have to shoot from the hip and trust in yourself to come through, one more time.

Years ago when my mother saw a baby do something really cute she'd say, "How precious!" And that word is perfect to describe those midnight moments with the babe-in-arms, moments when you know that something is being communicated to your child about his father's capacity to give warmth and comfort, something that will stay with that child and let him know that there's more to being a man than making money and women; there's the love communicated directly, the soft voice that says, "It's All Right," the holding that calms the stomach and soothes the soul.

They say that men are warlike creatures, that hormones rage in their veins and sweep them relentlessly toward the jails and divorce courts. They say they're shiftless, prideful and stubborn, knot-headed and hotheaded, greedy and vain. And maybe they're right—they probably are right, at least some of the time.

But maybe that's because men haven't marched with enough babies. Maybe if men marched with more babies they wouldn't want to march with as many armies.

Maybe men don't need to beat their swords into plowshares; as every farmer knows, plowing is hard, lonely work. It doesn't make you feel warm and fuzzy; it makes you sick and tired of plowing. So maybe instead of carrying more guns and pushing more plows, men need to march with more babies.

And it's happening; more and more men all over the world are reaching down into the crib in the middle of the night, feeling the oceanic sense of unity that comes when your offspring sleeps on your shoulder. Maybe it's making the men different; maybe it's making the babies different. Time will tell.

One thing is for sure: When the digital clock reads 3:17 A.M. and something gets you out of bed, it had better be precious.

And it is.

ABOUT THE AUTHOR
Dr. Michael J. Murphy

Michael Murphy, born in Springfield, Massachusetts, received his B.A. in Philosophy from Holy Cross College and his doctoral degree from East Texas State University in Commerce, Texas. He lived for ten years in rural Vermont, serving as a clinician and director of a community mental health center in North Adams, Massachusetts. Now living with his family in Cape Cod, Massachusetts, he works as a psychologist for the Department of Corrections at the Treatment Center in Bridgewater, Massachusetts; as a founding member of the Family Consultation Team, officed in Sagamore Beach, Massachusetts; and as adjunct faculty at Lesley College graduate school. Michael is licensed as a psychologist in Massachusetts and Vermont and is certified as a forensic psychologist. He is a clinical member and approved supervisor of the American Association for Marriage and Family Therapy. He has worked with men's groups for ten years and is himself the father of a blended family. He has received the Reilly Memorial Prize for outstanding creative writing, and his work has been included in an anthology of the best of the award-winning *Family Therapy Networker* magazine, and in the best-selling book *Chicken Soup for the Soul*.

ABOUT THE ILLUSTRATOR
Susanna Hepburn Kravitz

Susanna Hepburn Kravitz lives on a Connecticut mountaintop with her husband Robert; children, Jarrett, Naomi, Owen and Olivia; polka-dotted Newfoundlands, Toby and Tugboat; and canary Pizza Face. Her minutes on the planet are spent deeply immersed in children's athletic events, gardening, and creating artwork for galleries of the East Coast. Sue's love of art, nature, and family was nurtured by her parents through weekly family hikes and years spent watching her father build his stone wall along a brook. She is currently working on illustrating a children's book.

The Family Consultation Team

Through The Family Consultation Team, Michael strives to support fathering and to serve families and other systems in the process of transition. Loving and empowered fathers are the key solution to the problem of violence and the creation of the safety essential to the healthy development of children. In support of fathering and the healthy handling of change, the Team offers the following services:

- Fathering Workshops—Half-day or full-day intensive workshops on the background and importance of fathering.
- EnGendering Resolutions—Organizational consultation and training centered around the creative management of conflict.
- Family Consultation—Intensive team consultation for families in the process of developmental transition.

If we can be of service to you, your family, or your organization, please contact us.

For further information call 1-508-833-3800,

or write to:

The Family Consultation Team
349 Old Plymouth Road
P.O. Box 300
Sagamore Beach, MA 02562